SOME PARADES NEED RAIN

SOME PARADES NEED RAIN

A ROAD MAP TO RECONCILIATION IN

STRIFE-TORN TIMES

JON IVEY

CONTENTS

CHAPTER 1: TO WHACK OR NOT TO WHACK 9

CHAPTER 2: THE ROVE DUBYA AXIS OF MASS DECEPTION 14

CHAPTER 3: A GODLY NATION 31

CHAPTER 4 : POLITICAL QUIETISM:
                 ENEMY OF THE WHORE OF BABYLON 66

CHAPTER 5: IS GOD ANTI-SEMITIC? 77

CHAPTER 6: WHO ARE GOD'S CHILDREN? 85

CHAPTER 7: THE MINISTRY OF RECONCILIATION TODAY 90

CHAPTER 8: TWICE MORE INTO THE BREACH 103

CHAPTER 9: WHY I LEFT THE REPUBLICAN PARTY 110

CHAPTER 10: CONCLUDING SPIRITUAL SUBTEXT 113

ENDNOTES 125

Contents

In Memoriam, Paul Eugene Ivey.
February 9, 1928-March 25, 2003.
Rest in peace, Daddy.

CHAPTER 1

TO WHACK OR NOT TO WHACK

David lived in fear for his life because King Saul had ordered his murder, despite being—or perhaps because he was—God's designated successor to the throne. After all, Saul was jealous of the young upstart's fame when he sank a lethal surprise into Goliath's forehead. But as it turned out, a golden opportunity was handed to David when the king chose the very cave to move his bowels in where the fugitive was hiding. It might come as a surprise to many that he decided not to assassinate him. Why not? It was self-defense, wasn't it? "He said to his men, 'The Lord forbid that I should do such a thing to my master, the Lord's anointed, or lift my hand against him; for he is the anointed of the Lord.' With these words David rebuked his men and did not allow them to attack Saul" (I Samuel 24:6-7). A scholar expands on a theme that must seem quaint to modern ears:

> "Why did men consider the anointed to be inviolate, to be kept from attack, and to be preserved from degradation? The answer lies in the fact that once anointed, the individual was set apart or consecrated to God. A specific bond was established in relation to God, in separation from men and women in general, and from the common aspects of life in particular . . . . Hence to touch, defile, and attack the anointed one was to approach the Lord himself and to seek to defile, harm, and remove the Lord from his rightful place"[1].

David's followers were mustard keen to take Saul out right there in the cave. What an opportunity! To thwart their bloodlust "the Hebrew text reads 'so David 'tore apart' his men with the words', suggesting that David had to resort to violent and threatening language" against them[2].

Although he'd already been promised the kingdom, he knew the end doesn't justify the means. Far be it from him to act so godlessly! "Yahweh's will must be achieved in Yahweh's way; the end that God has ordained must be reached by the means that God approves"[3]. It's normal for a worldly man to seek a shortcut when faced with a similar situation, but Jesus' response when Satan offered him all the kingdoms of the world if he'd only fall down and worship him is instructive. "Jesus said to him, 'Away from me, Satan! For it is written: Worship the Lord your God, and serve him only'" (Matthew 4:10).

I wouldn't take President Bush to task so severely if he weren't a professing Christian. I'm concerned that Muslims and other non-Christians might mistakenly infer that violence, deceit and self-righteousness is the Christian way. *Au contraire*. The Prince of Peace says to us today "Blessed are the peacemakers, for they will be called sons of God" (Matthew 5:9). "Blessed are the poor in spirit, for theirs is the kingdom of heaven. Blessed are those who mourn, for they will be comforted. Blessed are the meek, for they will inherit the earth" (verses 3-5). "Finally, all of you, live in harmony with one another; be sympathetic, love as brothers, be compassionate and humble . . . . For whoever would love life and see good days must keep his tongue from evil and his lips from deceitful speech. He must turn from evil and do good; he must seek peace and pursue it. For the eyes of the Lord are on the righteous and his ears are attentive to their prayer, but the face of the Lord is against those who do evil" (I Peter 3:8ff.). "Humble yourselves, therefore, under God's mighty hand, that he may lift you up in due time" (I Peter 5:6). How did Jesus deal with suffering? "Christ suffered for you, leaving you an example, that you should follow in his steps. He committed no sin, and no deceit was found in his mouth. When they hurled their insults at him, he did not retaliate; when he suffered, he made no threats. Instead, he entrusted himself to him who judges justly" (I Peter 2:21-23). "Do not repay anyone evil for evil. Be careful to do what is right in the eyes of everybody. If it is possible, as far as it depends on you, live at peace with everyone. Do not take revenge, my friends, but leave room for God's wrath, for it is written: It is mine to avenge; I will repay, says the Lord. On the contrary: If your enemy is hungry, feed him; if he is thirsty, give him something to drink. In doing this, you will heap burning coals on his head. Do not be overcome by evil, but overcome evil with good" (Romans 12:17ff.). If this applies to our sworn enemies in Al Qaeda, how much more so to countries like Iraq that aren't after us but are attacked without cause.

> "Consider John Murray's perceptive comment on Romans 12:19 (also apropos the situation in I Samuel 24): 'Here we have what belongs to the essence of piety. The essence of ungodliness is that we presume to take the place of God, to take everything into our own hands. It is faith to commit ourselves to God, to cast all our care upon him and to vest all our interests in him. In reference to the matter in hand, the wrongdoing of which we are the victims, the way of faith is to recognize that God is judge and to leave the execution of vengeance and retribution to him"[4].

But not only are Christians forbidden to pursue vengeance, there's an additional divine command against regime change generally. The Apostle Paul writes: "Everyone must submit himself to the governing authorities, for there is no authority except that which God has established. The authorities that exist have been established by God. Consequently, he who rebels against the authority is rebelling against what God has instituted, and those who do so will bring judgment on themselves . . . . For [the ruler] is God's servant to do you good. But if you do wrong, be afraid, for he does not bear the sword for nothing. He is God's servant, an agent of justice to bring punishment on the wrongdoer" (Romans 13:1ff.). A Bible commentary says: "The man in authority may be unworthy, but the institution is not, since God wills it"[5]. Both text and context make it abundantly clear that Paul has all governing authorities in mind here. Note the universal nature of the following sentence: "for there is no authority except that which God has established". Those who rebel against the authorities bring judgment on themselves, "For God is not a God of disorder but of peace" (I Corinthians 14:33). Jesus sternly warned those who use force to right wrongs. While he—an innocent man!—was being arrested, a friend of his cut off the high priest's servant's ear. "'Put your sword back in its place,' Jesus said to him, 'for all who draw the sword will die by the sword'" (Matthew 26:52). And as Hannah Arendt suggests, the "practice of violence, like all action, changes the world, but the most probable change is to a more violent world"[6].

When Saul issued the order to murder David, his own son rebuked him to his face. "Let not the king do wrong to his servant David; he has not wronged you, and what he has done has benefited you greatly. He took his life in his hands when he killed [Goliath]. The Lord won a great victory for all Israel, and you saw it and were glad. Why then would you do wrong to an innocent man like David by killing him for no reason?" (I Samuel 19:4-5).

Many years ago, when the US government decided on regime change in Iraq, the CIA helped Saddam Hussein gain power. During the Reagan presidency, millions of our tax dollars helped Hussein in his war with Iran because it was thought at the time that Khomeini's kind of Islam represented a graver threat to our interests than did Hussein. And Defense Secretary Rumsfeld has made threatening noises about the prospect of a future Iraq dominated by Shia Muslims. Seen in this light, didn't Hussein's suppression of a Shia uprising in 1991, a rebellion that the first Pres. Bush encouraged, make that prospect more remote? Taking all these things into consideration, a plausible case can be made that Hussein has assisted the stated objectives of our government. And although he has threatened and even harmed his neighbors, he hasn't massed his troops on our borders or dropped dirty bombs on our cities. And Al Qaeda attacked us on September 11, not Hussein. David complained to Saul during an interlude in the chase: "I have not wronged you, but you are hunting me down to take my life" (I Samuel 24:11). Sadly, it seems that when we threaten countries like Iran (to take one example) and they take defensive measures, we even claim the dubious right to interpret their moves as cause for harming them. What a staggering burden on one's conscience is needless bloodshed!

If Pres. Bush is a Christian, he should heed the exhortation of the Apostle Peter: "make every effort to add to your faith goodness; and to goodness, knowledge; and to knowledge, self-control; and to self-control, perseverance; and to perseverance, godliness; and to godliness, brotherly kindness; and to brotherly kindness, love. For if you possess these qualities in increasing measure, they will keep you from being ineffective and unproductive in your knowledge of our Lord Jesus Christ. But if anyone does not have them, he is nearsighted and blind, and has forgotten that he has been cleansed from his past sins" (II Peter 1:5-9).

The mark of a Christian is a desire to obey God's voice. In another context, prior to David's encounter with Goliath, the Lord rebuked Saul for his disobedience as follows: "Does the Lord delight in burnt offerings and sacrifices as much as in obeying the voice of the Lord? To obey is better than sacrifice, and to heed is better than the fat of rams. For rebellion is like the sin of divination, and arrogance like the evil of idolatry. Because you have rejected the word of the Lord, he has rejected you as king" (I Samuel 15:22-23).

God's anger burns against those who treat with contempt something or someone set apart or consecrated to him. When an Israelite brought a sacrifice to the house of the Lord, the wicked sons of Eli the priest would ask for some of the meat. The sin was not in the request itself, as they were entitled to a share, but in demanding that if it wasn't handed over immediately, they'd take it by force. "This sin of the young men was very great in the Lord's sight, for they were treating the Lord's offering with contempt" (I Samuel 2:17). As with offerings set apart to God, so with governing authorities, all of whom have been ordained or set apart by God (Romans 13:1).

It has been dinned into our ears countless times by Republicans that no man is above the law. Yet scorn and malicious abuse are heaped on the head of anyone who invokes this dictum in calling George W. Bush to account. How different Bill Clinton's second term would've turned out if *his* supporters had cowed the Republicans into submission by showering them with vicious and vituperative insults. (Talk show host Sean Hannity listened approvingly while a celebrity caller described 85-year-old Senator Robert Byrd as a punk. I heard this with my own ears). By intimidating and hectoring and interrupting them, he might have avoided the public humiliation over Monica Lewinsky, not to mention the marital discord and millions in legal expenses over Whitewater and other bogus accusations. Do the children of Republicans walk up to the TV set when Bush is on the screen and exclaim "Bad man!" as they draw an X across his image? I guess some men are above the law after all.

CHAPTER 2

THE ROVE DUBYA AXIS OF MASS DECEPTION

"Live as children of light (for the fruit of the light consists in all goodness, righteousness and truth) and find out what pleases the Lord. Have nothing to do with the fruitless deeds of darkness, but rather expose them" (Ephesians 5:8-11).

The Big Lie is that aggression is self-defense. But these are contraries, much like light and darkness, good and evil, mercy and judgment. "Woe to those who call evil good and good evil, who put darkness for light and light for darkness, who put bitter for sweet and sweet for bitter" (Isaiah 5:20).

In Swift's tale, Gulliver finds it exceedingly difficult to explain the concept of lying to a bewildered Houyhnhnm, the latter protesting that "the Use of Speech was to make us understand one another, and to receive Information of Facts; now if anyone *said the Thing which was not*, these ends were defeated; because I cannot properly be said to understand him; and I am so far from receiving Information, that he leaves me worse than in Ignorance; for I am led to believe a Thing *Black* when it is *White*, and *Short* when it is *Long*"[7].

Russell Kirk, the sage of American conservatism, cites a comment by English jurist Sir James Fitzjames Stephen: "Words are tools which break in one's hand; put a powerful strain upon them, and an advantage is given in argument to the inferior thinker over the superior"[8]. And finally, there's an old song that says:

> While everyone clamors for the justice they seek
> The Word is corrupted and the strong take the weak.[9]

"In you are slanderous men bent on shedding blood" (Ezekiel 22:9).

On a great big hill there lurked a man and his bristling armory of lethal weapons. Qarl knew deep in his heart of hearts that he'd been born for such a time as this, that there'd never ever been a more urgent and dire need for applying his ministrations to a grateful world waiting expectantly and hanging on his every pronouncement. *They* knew that a protracted and complex crisis over which statesmen and politicos had butted heads and jabbed pudgy fingers into maps for decades quickly melted away whenever he consulted his almanac for background info and then focused that gifted and teeming mind of his on solving it.

But alas, no fans hovered around his front door seeking autographs. True, the world did hang on his words but not from admiration for his genius and perspicacity. For it was apparent to one and all that Qarl possessed a uniquely ferocious temper and the memory of an elephant, yes even a granddaddy elephant. Did someone foolishly oppose his efforts? Very well then, you are now to be hated intensely and permanently. Now there are those brave souls who can weather the stormy anger of an implacable foe, but did I mention his weapons of mass destruction?

On a tour of the armory, they say Ms Chaneyberry's second-grade class was ushered into an enormous hangar. When ropes were pulled and covers fell off of the fearsome weapons, six of the kids fainted dead away. Only one of these hailed from a Democrat home. But I wander.

Qarl need only fix a gimlet eye on a Middle Eastern sheikh actually— think of it!—criticizing him and plotting ways of thwarting him—how could anyone be so evil?!?!—and then disaster strikes. Qarl presses a button on his desk that launches a missile so swift and precise that our hapless sheikh's retinue can do nothing but reach out and grab his falling falafel and pita sandwich when, moments later, the lofty one meets his end.

With Qarl in a foul mood, his next-door neighbors dive for cover and even folks on the opposite side of his globe soil their shorts. His satellite dish went out one night during his favorite movie and so the neighbors, as nervous as a frog on a freeway with his hopper busted, kept shouting "It was the lightning. Be sweet! It wasn't us! We didn't do it! Honest, it's the lightning!"

Decades ago, a man with a large family got a vasectomy done but it didn't take so his corpulent wife got pregnant with number 24. Not realizing what was going on for those nine months—she was *that* fat— the birth so traumatized them both that they fell to drinking heavily. Fed up with the delay, someone in the hospital who'd fallen in love with her new ride named the lil' fella Sedan.

Now Sedan as a young boy grew into something of a control freak who enjoyed outwitting others, torturing critters large and small, and basking in adulation and praise. As you can well imagine, politics was the career path for him. In his neighborhood, there was the odd dustup with Wade and Ron. (Ron's swagger really ticked him off). But it certainly never crossed his mind that Qarl, who lived far away, would ever make things warm for him. Besides, he knew that Qarl's forebears had pestered their neighbors, so why couldn't he take advantage of his? Oh, and did I mention that Sedan lived on a rock?

One fine day, Qarl sat comfortably ensconced in his lair, munching on Funyuns and leafing through an encyclopedia, steaming coffee mug close by. The snail was on the thorn, as the poet said, and all seemed right with the world. Until the shocking and enraging news reached him that a devastating and deadly attack had just been perpetrated on his own citadel by zealots from some distant place called Soddy or Rocco or something like that. In days to come, he'd sit at times with fingers entwined behind his head and recall with a modicum of self-satisfaction that, just prior to the dastardly deed, he'd learned from a book that this notion of an 'eye rack' was just a crock. Many people didn't realize that, he would think, but *he* did. But of course there was precious little time for reflection in those frightful days, for his spies had fingered a culprit who went by the nickname Sammy Ben.

Now obviously when Sedan read in the papers that The Glare had turned fully to face Sammy Ben, he experienced a flood of relief akin to that felt by a fleeing shoplifter who finds himself overtaken and then passed by cops chasing a bank robber ahead of him. He wouldn't be bothered as he continued his troublemaking. Or so he thought. But so many people were so incensed by the highhandedness of those who dwelt on the hilltop that Sammy Ben managed to elude his fleet-footed pursuers.

So, like a tractor trailer with headlights set on high beam, The Glare swiveled back around onto Sedan, who found things getting warm for himself after all. Nervously he surveyed his arsenal and found only a warehouse or two filled with tiny Soviet tanks minus the treads, shoulder-fired RPGs, old-timey MIGs without those cockpit canopies that keep the wind off, and a crate of pop guns stenciled with the words: "CIA: It is a violation of Federal law to use this product in a manner inconsistent with its labeling." In a blue funk and feeling—for once in his life—powerless, he cast about in his mind what he should do. Just then his sons Booday and Noosay staggered in from a late night shindig, reminiscing dreamily on account of a certain chemical, whereupon a light went on in Sedan's noggin. He placed a phone call.

Now in a normal world peopled by midgets, a lone giant who had a notion to do something would just do it. You'd be lounging there in your hut minding your own business and clipping your tiny nails when, after a brief shadow outside, a huge foot would come slamming down on top of you, obliterating you and yours. And if a neighbor had the audacity to question the giant, why he'd just stare at you for a while until you got good and nauseous and then clear his throat ominously, curl his lip and growl "Because I said so." Curiously though, Qarl wasn't like that. Instead he'd just make fervent speeches about patriotism and some mysterious ogre he called Tare and his publicity department would then swing into action, cranking out gung-ho analyses of heartrending video clips showing the aftermath when Tare had struck, but leaving out the events that led up to it. Sort of like when an obnoxious patron in a movie theater keeps doing annoying things like eating your popcorn or fondling your date or yakking loudly on your cellphone and then you object somewhat coldly and so he leans into your personal space, his countenance radiating hatred and self-righteousness of alarming intensity, and spits out some such accusation as "You HATE me, don't you?"

And so we were told with a straight face that although Sammy Ben hasn't been picked up yet, we've detected a secret meeting between his people and Sedan's and so we're going to have to kick hiney and take names. But if Hitler's folk got together with Stalin's for a friendly chat, does this mean Stalin is responsible for the Holocaust? Nevertheless, like the preacher's note to himself in the margin of his sermon: "logic weak here. shout louder," publicity keeps banging on incessantly and incoherently about Tare and patriotic duty and how if you study Sammy Ben's name carefully and squint hard enough it can look like Sammy Dan or Sam Dan or even Sedan. And for the critics there were the emotionally charged tie-down questions: "You just don't get it, do you?" "You believe in the war on Tare, don't you?" "Our children shouldn't have to live in fear, should they?" "You like the way Sedan runs things, don't you?" "You're just a yellowbellied pacifist, aren't you?" "Admit it, you really deep down in your heart want Qarl to get the heave-ho, don't you?" "You ARE a patriot, AREN'T you?"

Meanwhile, in a secret location a man named Ollie watches with sadistic glee as two quadraplegics bite down on and squirt deadly toxin capsules on each other. The phone rings. When Sedan learns that the chemical and biological weapons have all been destroyed by a relative of his and when Ollie also informs him that the delivery vehicles necessary for striking an enemy have been secretly sold by a subordinate to feed his starving brood, Sedan is enraged and shoots up some furniture.

Now if aggression is self-defense, one might conjecture that the converse is true, too. Self-defense is aggression. Hence the supposed existence of Saddam Hussein's weapons, along with his use of them to defend himself against rebels, was seized upon to justify attack. Gulliver explains to a puzzled Houyhnhnm one of the causes of this strange thing called war. "Sometimes one Prince quarrelleth with another, for fear the other should quarrel with him"[10]. Curiously though, when Abe Lincoln and Andrew Jackson fill mass graves with rebels and neighbors, their birthdays are celebrated and their portraits grace the currency. And when the US is attacked, that's NOT self-defense. I guess it's true what they say. I don't get it, after all.

"Do not plot harm against your neighbor . . . . Do not accuse a man for no reason—when he has done you no harm" (Proverbs 3:29-30). "Warn a divisive person once, and then warn him a second time. After that, have nothing to do with him. You may be sure that such a man is warped and sinful; he is self-condemned" (Titus 3:10-11).

Another lie we often heard was that any criticism of the invasion of

Iraq was politically, intellectually and/or morally deficient. Thus the critics were smeared as partisan, politically ambitious, unpatriotic, traitors, appeasers, slow-witted, cowardly, pacifist, socialist or punks among many other terms of abuse and character assassination. "But mark this: There will be terrible times in the last days. People will be ... boastful, proud, abusive, ... unholy, without love, unforgiving, slanderous, ... brutal, ... treacherous, rash, conceited ... having a form of godliness but denying its power. Have nothing to do with them" (II Timothy 3:1-5).

I suppose if a thought is repeated over and over, many people acquiesce in believing it without applying critical intelligence to the matter. For instance, the neo-conservatives in the Bush Administration are conservatives. (How does *that* old chestnut grab you?) If so, then why do they share so many traits with the totalitarians who crushed and gobbled up Europe last century, such as "the purificatory function of death, the conception of a moral vanguard, the call to direct action, the dream of a purified world"[11]? One might also mention the sense of absolute certainty the movement feels about its ideals and mission, reminiscent of Lenin, which justifies—in their own twisted thinking—the brutal verbal abuse and aggressive violence it showers on those brave souls who oppose them. For these reasons, let us reclaim the word 'conservatism' from those who would profane it and rename those Administration officials with a term at once memorable and truly descriptive. Ladies and gentlemen, I present to you the neo-Bolsheviks.

For what is the true meaning of the word 'conservatism'? Allow Russell Kirk, author of *The Conservative Mind from Burke to Eliot*, to weigh in with some of his "canons of conservative thought":

> "Belief in a transcendent order, or body of natural law, which rules society as well as conscience. Political problems, at bottom, are religious and moral problems ... True politics is the art of apprehending and applying the Justice which ought to prevail in a community of souls ....

> Affection for the proliferating variety and mystery of human existence, as opposed to the narrowing uniformity ... of most radical systems.

Faith in prescription and distrust of 'sophisters, calculators, and economists' who would reconstruct society upon abstract designs . . . Conservatives respect the wisdom of their ancestors . . . Custom, convention, and old prescription are checks both upon man's anarchic impulse and upon the innovator's lust for power.

Recognition that change may not be salutary reform: hasty innovation may be a devouring conflagration, rather than a torch of progress . . . they are dubious of wholesale alteration. They think society is a spiritual reality, possessing an eternal life but a delicate constitution: it cannot be scrapped and recast as if it were a machine . . . Society must alter, for prudent change is the means of social preservation; but a statesman must take Providence into his calculations, and a statesman's chief virtue, according to Plato and Burke, is prudence"[12].

It is actually claimed, with a degree of credulity normally found only in cultists, that George W. Bush has raised the moral tone relative to his predecessor. Calf slobber. Why was Senator McCain, co-author of a campaign finance reform bill, not even invited to the presidential signing ceremony? In Queen Noor's memoirs, she tells the story of a general who tried to overthrow her husband, Jordan's King Hussein. Not only was the rebel forgiven, but he was later appointed Ambassador to France[13]. The Bible says "the Lord's servant must not quarrel; instead, he must be kind to everyone, . . . not resentful" (II Timothy 2:24).

Many times in the years since 9/11, Bush proclaimed that he will hunt down the terrorists and that the US will prevail. "Now listen, you who say, 'Today or tomorrow we will go to this or that city, spend a year there, carry on business and make money.' Why, you do not even know what will happen tomorrow. What is your life? You are a mist that appears for a little while and then vanishes. Instead, you ought to say, 'If it is the Lord's will, we will live and do this or that.' As it is, you boast and brag. All such boasting is evil" (James 4:13-16).

According to Mehmet Dulger, chairman of the Turkish Parliament's

Foreign Affairs Committee, the way the US tried to gain approval for opening a northern front against Iraq was—how shall I put this?—harsh and rude. Mr Dulger complained that his people were badmouthed as "rug merchants" and "bellydancers" and that the Americans had "refused to listen to Turkish concerns." When Yashar Yakis, the foreign minister, told the President of his government's serious reservations about acceding to all the American proposals, he was brushed off with the words: "I understand, but now go back to Turkey and do the job"[14]. One attribute of the Christian character, according to Galatians 5:22, is patience. "But the fruit of the Spirit is love, joy, peace, patience, kindness, goodness, faithfulness, gentleness and self-control." In a commentary on the book of Galatians we read that patience is "the quality of putting up with others, even when one is severely tried. The importance of patience is evidenced by its being most often used of the character of God, as in the great text from Joel"[15]. "Return to the Lord your God, for he is gracious and compassionate, *slow to anger* and abounding in love, and he relents from sending calamity" (Joel 2:13). Was Bush patient and gentle with the Turks?

Galatians 5:19-21 throws Christian character into sharp relief by contrast as follows: "The acts of the sinful nature are obvious: . . . hatred, discord, . . . fits of rage, selfish ambition . . ." Hatred means "'enmities' such as those between classes, nations [what's that about 'cheese-eating surrender monkeys'?], and individuals . . . . 'fits of rage' can denote both good and bad qualities. There is a godly zeal as well as righteous anger. When zeal or anger originate from selfish motives and hurt pride, they are evil and harm others . . . . 'Selfish ambition' may be translated in many ways: contention, strife, selfishness, rivalry, intrigues. Its basic meaning is a selfish and self-aggrandizing approach to work"[16]. In our relations with France, we can also find evidence of malice, defined by another commentator as "a mind-set that attributes evil motives to others without provocation"[17].

If Bill Clinton was rash and heedless in sexual matters, his successor was rash and reckless with people's lives. Republican Sen. Richard Lugar complained that the planning phase for postwar Iraq "started very late . . . . A gap has occurred, and that has brought some considerable suffering"[18]. And unlike Clinton, Bush is a warmonger. Administration officials informed military planners shortly after September 11 of their 'hit list' (my term) of six more countries they wanted to take out. Syria, Iran, Lebanon, Somalia, Sudan and Libya were shoved into the bull's eye to bear the brunt of neo-Bolshevik violence[19]. (Recently Libya has reformed its ways and thus might very well evade The Glare). A Middle East expert named Dilip Hiro warns that our "refusal, whether in Pakistan, Cairo, or Gaza, to recognize the connection between politics and terror, between grievance and the violence it provokes . . . sets the United States 'on an inexorable course of war without end'"[20]. The importance of peace in the Christian life is clear from its ubiquity in the New Testament. The word appears eighty times and in every book[21]. "Make every effort [note the emphatic nature of the command] to live in peace with all men" (Hebrews 12:14).

We will certainly never see George Bush wagging his finger and declaring on camera that he did NOT have sex with that intelligence report, nor in my opinion should we. And whether it should've been parsed so thoroughly is an open question. But I can say with confidence that the effect of organizing a bespoke spy ring, when the regular spooks weren't saying what Secretary Rumsfeld wanted to hear, in order to finger Iraq as a terrorist state, is unsettling[22].

And as to the allegation that Iraq had a hand in bringing down the World Trade Center and the other two planes, Thomas Powers, author of *Intelligence Wars: American Secret History from Hitler to al-Qaeda*, categorically declares: "The United States and Britain never found any connection between Iraq and the attacks of September 11"[23].

The trump card in the President's hand was national security. Because of his sincere concern for national security, many Americans still considered him the best man for the job. But according to a CNN report in August 2003, fishermen who came ashore near JFK Airport were able to wander unmolested on airport property for over an hour. Almost two years after the terrorist attacks, they were not only never challenged as they walked near the runways, but airport personnel didn't even know they were there until the trespassers approached them for assistance in getting home. Think of the damage a terrorist standing near a runway could cause with a single shoulder-fired missile.

An interview with Isaac Yeffet, former head of global security for El Al Airlines and founder of an airline security consultancy, was published in the September 2003 issue of Technology Review magazine. His analysis of US airport security is not encouraging. He stated that the baggage screeners "are not qualified, and the technology we have at the airports around the country—which has a 35 percent false-alarm rate—is the wrong concept . . . [This] comes to between 1.2 and 1.3 million pieces of luggage a day that we have to rescreen or hand search. Now this is wrong, because you cannot drive the screeners crazy by [making them open] luggage after luggage to find out there is no explosive. One of the biggest enemies of security is routine. After a while, it becomes a routine, and the screeners will not pay attention anymore. They are not even trained to do a professional hand search, especially when we deal with a sophisticated enemy who knows how to conceal explosives in a double bottom." Although Yeffet praises the security offered by Continental Airlines on its flights from Newark to Tel Aviv and Amsterdam, overall his assessment is scathingly critical[24].

A French king famously declared "L'etat c'est moi." In this country we don't have a tradition of identifying a nation with a ruler's interests so closely, so it's not at all unpatriotic to ask whether Bush's foreign policy will enhance security or not. In his letter of resignation to his boss Colin Powell on the eve of the invasion, career diplomat John Brady Kiesling protests that "[t]he policies we are now asked to advance are incompatible not only with American values but also with American interests . . . Have we indeed become blind, as Russia is blind in Chechnya, as Israel is blind in the Occupied Territories, to *our own advice*, that overwhelming military power is not the answer to terrorism"[25]? He also writes that "the more aggressively we use our power to intimidate our foes, the more foes we create and the more we validate terrorism as the only effective weapon of the powerless against the powerful"[26].

One of the things that most distressed me about the rationale proffered in support of the invasion was that we could easily find ourselves hoist with our own petar. The historian Polybius relates an encounter with Roman general Scipio after he'd defeated Carthage. As Scipio stood watching the city aflame, "Polybius asked the general why he repeated [certain words of triumph] in so tender a manner, in the midst of his success against enemies? Scipio answered, that in viewing the destruction of Carthage, he contemplated the uncertainty of empire, with a foreboding apprehension, that the most prosperous, might some time or other share the same fate"[27]. Or as Prof. Stanley Hoffmann puts it a bit more prosaically:

> "[A] pure and simple return to the rule of the strongest would be a catastrophic regression. It would promote insecurity, not security or moderation. Those who approved of the war in Iraq for entirely understandable reasons of humanitarianism, of pity for the Iraqi people, and of horror at Saddam Hussein's regime seldom considered that a precedent used for a 'good' cause can easily be used by others for causes they would object to: Russia could use it against Georgia, India against Pakistan, North Korea against South Korea"[28]. One might also add that Al Qaeda could use it against us because, in their eyes, we aren't righteous. A scholar of Islam chillingly predicts that "if the [Muslim fundamentalists] can persuade the world of Islam to accept their views and their leadership, then a long and bitter struggle lies ahead, and not only for America"[29].

Speaking of unsettling news, David Corn wrote a story in the August 4, 2003 issue of *The Nation* that describes White House retaliation against US ambassador Joe Wilson, whose trip to Africa the previous year failed to turn up sufficient evidence of Saddam Hussein's supposed attempts to purchase materials useful for producing nuclear weapons. Displeased with Wilson's report, White House officials outed his wife as a CIA agent, in violation of federal law. If the President cared so deeply about national security, why would her identity be revealed given that her expertise is in counterterrorism?

The Rove Dubya Axis busily beavered away at its work. Here are four more of its deceptions. First, Resolution 1441 was not grounds for an attack on Iraq for, as Dr. Hoffmann points out, it was vague enough to allow for conflicting interpretations. Indeed both the US and France claimed that its adoption vindicated their respective policies[30]. Second, France didn't deserve our anathema. Hoffmann complains that none of the US print or broadcast media that he's seen accurately described the French government's position on Iraq. Indeed

> "it was not a journalist, but the dean of the Woodrow Wilson School at Princeton, Anne-Marie Slaughter, who revealed in the *Washington Post* on April 13, 2003, that the French ambassador to Washington had relayed to the administration a French proposal that could have avoided the bitter Franco-American break: the US would have given up the idea of proposing a second resolution (which it finally had to withdraw since there weren't enough votes for it), and France and the US would have 'agreed to disagree'. This would have made the threat of a French veto unnecessary, and allowed the US to proceed with its war and to invoke resolution 1441 as a basis for it. But Bush preferred a public showdown on a second resolution which Tony Blair needed at home. It preferred helping Blair, a loyal ally, to a deal with Chirac, a dissenting and thus lapsed ally"[31].

Hoffmann also cites Chirac's appearance on 60 Minutes on March 16, 2003 , in which he told Christiane Amanpour that if "our strategy, inspections, were failing, we would consider all the options, including war"[32].

New York University's Tony Judt offers some needed historical perspective on the question of French cowardice.

> "In World War I, which the French fought from start to finish, France lost three times as many fighting men as America has lost in all its wars combined. In World War II, the French armies holding off the Germans in May-June 1940 suffered 124,000 dead and 200,000 wounded in six weeks, more than America did in Korea and Vietnam combined. Until Hitler brought the US into the war against him in December 1941, Washington maintained correct diplomatic relations with the Nazi regime. Meanwhile the *Einsatzgruppen* had been at work for six months slaughtering Jews on the Eastern Front, and the Resistance was active in occupied France.

Fortunately we shall never know how middle America would have responded if instructed by an occupying power to persecute racial minorities in its midst. But even in the absence of such mitigating circumstances the precedents are not comforting—remember the Tulsa pogrom of May 1921, when at least 350 blacks were killed by whites. Perhaps, too, Americans should hesitate before passing overhasty judgments about 'age-old' French anti-Semitism: by the end of the nineteenth century France's elite École Normale Supérieure was admitting (by open competition) brilliant young Jews— Léon Blum, Emile Durkheim, Henri Bergson, Daniel Halévy, and dozens of others—who would never have been allowed near some of America's Ivy League colleges, then and for decades to come"[33].

Third, those around the world who opposed our foreign policy in the past few years were mostly not motivated by anti-Americanism. We turn again to Hoffmann's essay. "The anti-Americanism on the rise throughout the world is not just hostility toward the most powerful nation, or based on the old clichés of the left and the right; nor is it only envy or hatred of our values. It is, more often than not, a resentment of double standards and double talk, of crass ignorance and arrogance, of wrong assumptions and dubious policies"[34].

Fourth, contrary to the pernicious propaganda emanating from the Axis, Europe is not boiling over with anti-Semitism. Tony Judt analyzes in detail an interesting report on the topic by the American Anti-Defamation League (ADL), which found 45 significant anti-Semitic incidents in 2002 in France, but "60 anti-Semitic incidents on US college campuses alone in 1999 . . . there is no evidence to suggest [these incidents are] more widespread in Europe than in the US"[35]. As for the issue of Jewish loyalties,

"it is 'Americans', not Europeans, who are readier to assume that a Jew's first loyalty might be to Israel. The ADL and most American commentators conclude from this that there is no longer any difference between being 'against' Israel and 'against' Jews. But this is palpably false. The highest level of pro-Palestinian sympathy in Europe today is recorded in

Denmark, a country which also registers as one of the least anti-Semitic *by the ADL's own criteria*. Another country with a high and increasing level of sympathy for the Palestinians is the Netherlands; yet the Dutch have the lowest anti-Semitic 'quotient' in Europe and nearly half of them are 'worried' about the possible rise of anti-Semitism . . . Overall, Europeans are more likely to blame Israel than Palestinians for the present morass in the Middle East, but only by a ratio of 27:20. Americans, by contrast, blame Palestinians rather than Israel in the proportion of 42:17. This suggests that Europeans' responses are considerably more balanced, which is what one would expect: the European [media] provide a fuller and fairer coverage of events [there] than is available to most Americans[36]. As a consequence, Europeans are better than Americans at distinguishing criticism of Israel from dislike of Jews . . . The gap separating Europeans from Americans on the question of Israel and the Palestinians is the biggest impediment to transatlantic understanding today . . . On a 'warmth' scale of 1-100, American feelings toward Israel rate 55, whereas the European average is just 38- and somewhat cooler among the 'New Europeans': revealingly, the British and French give Israel the same score. It is the 'Poles' who exhibit by far the coolest feelings toward Israel (Donald Rumsfeld please note)[37].

In addition, we were led to believe that, simultaneously, Iraq will be recast in a Western-style liberal democratic mold favorable toward America, while we somehow move the region in the direction of moderation in dealing with Israel. I don't claim that this is a deliberate deception. More likely is that what we have here is typical American optimism, the gung-ho can-do spirit for which we're so famous. In this connection, I'm reminded of the narrator's remark in Graham Greene's *The Quiet American*: "I never knew a man who had better motives for all the trouble he caused." A plausible outcome is, on the contrary, a more intense hostility toward us and Israel because of nationalist, populist and religious factors[38].

Another troubling aspect of the Axis was media manipulation. The diplomat Kiesling writes, "[w]e have not seen such systematic distortion of intelligence, such systematic manipulation of American opinion, since the war in Vietnam"[39]. Brilliantly manipulating our fears, Bush was able to "increase his, and his country's, power. All that was needed was, first, to proclaim that we were at war (something other societies attacked by terrorists have not done), second, to extend that war to states sheltering or aiding terrorist groups, and third, to allege connections between Islamist terrorists and 'rogue states', such as Iraq and Iran, engaged in efforts to obtain or build weapons of mass terror . . . The case against Iraq's regime was at first based on stoking American fears about hidden weapons of mass destruction (while downplaying fears that North Korean nuclear bombs might provoke). When it became clear that Saddam Hussein's ability to threaten American security had been much exaggerated since the weapons proved hard to find, and the possession by Iraq of nuclear weapons was effectively denied by the UN inspectors, the reason for the war was shifted to human rights and democracy"[40]. Another technique was a resort to Orwellian rhetoric. The President told Americans that the war was not a policy chosen among others, but a necessity imposed by Saddam. Nations that resisted the administration's rush to war were presented as hostile for reasons of greed or of an incurable anti-Americanism[41].

A glaring example of White House manipulation was the manner in which it announced the formation of the Department of Homeland Security. Frank Rich writes: "Just hours before the FBI agent Colleen Rowley was to testify about her agency's catastrophic sloppiness in the weeks prior to 9/11, the White House abruptly announced its approval of a Department of Homeland Security, a Democratic idea it had previously fought. Rowley and her testimony soon disappeared from prominent view as the networks busily began publicizing the *pro forma* presidential address hastily assembled for prime-time airing that night"[42].

A young Republican activist named Jim Wilkinson was rewarded for his assistance during the Florida ballot recount in the 2000 election with a job as head of the Coalition Media Center in Doha, Qatar. Michael Massing, a contributing editor of the *Columbia Journalism Review*, traveled to Qatar on behalf of the Committee to Protect Journalists, of which he is a member of the board of directors. He reports that Wilkinson "was known to rebuke reporters whose copy he deemed insufficiently supportive of the war; he darkly warned one correspondent that he was on a 'list' along with two other reporters at his paper"[43].

For an article he wrote entitled "Fortress Bush" in the January 19, 2004 issue of *The New Yorker*, Ken Auletta talked to *Washington Post* White House correspondent Dana Milbank about a front page piece Milbank wrote (October 22, 2002) about White House deceit in the runup to the Iraq war. "According to Auletta, Milbank's article had in fact 'enraged' the White House, and several top Bush officials had complained to *Post* national editor Maralee Schwartz about Milbank, suggesting that he 'might be the wrong person for the job.' Milbank himself told Auletta that the White House tried to freeze him out and for a while stopped returning his calls"[44].

US journalists colluded with their manipulators in many ways. CNN even went to the trouble of setting up a separate news operation, offering to virgin American ears a "highly sanitized" portrayal of the war, a sort of less filling CNN Lite, in addition to their regular CNN International broadcast. Massing concluded that mostly "US news organizations gave Americans the war they thought Americans wanted to see". Journalist Russell Smith charged US TV stations with being "cravenly submissive to the Pentagon and the White House"[45]. At his prewar press conference, "not one of the sixteen journalists who asked questions about Iraq challenged him" when the President claimed a link between Iraq and Al Qaeda. It almost seemed at times that "the press had become 'embedded' not only in the fighting forces but in Washington officialdom itself"[46].

Call me an idealist if you will, but the proper relationship between citizen and ruler shouldn't be that of an unprincipled support. When King David committed adultery with Bathsheba and had her husband rubbed out,

> "the Lord sent Nathan to David. When he came to him, he said, 'There were two men in a certain town, one rich and the other poor. The rich man had a very large number of sheep and cattle, but the poor man had nothing except one little ewe lamb he had bought. He raised it, and it grew up with him and his children. It shared his food, drank from his cup and even slept in his arms. It was like a daughter to him.

Now a traveler came to the rich man, but the rich man refrained from taking one of his own sheep or cattle to prepare a meal for the traveler who had come to him. Instead, he took the ewe lamb that belonged to the poor man and prepared it for the one who had come to him.' David burned with anger against the man and said to Nathan, 'As surely as the Lord lives, the man who did this deserves to die! He must pay for that lamb four times over, because he did such a thing and had no pity.' Then Nathan said to David, 'You are the man! This is what the Lord, the God of Israel, says: 'I anointed you king over Israel, and I delivered you from the hand of Saul. I gave your master's house to you, and your master's wives into your arms. I gave you the house of Israel and Judah. And if all this had been too little, I would have given you even more. Why did you despise the word of the Lord by doing what is evil in his eyes? You struck down Uriah the Hittite with the sword and took his wife to be your own. You killed him with the sword of the Ammonites. Now, therefore, the sword will never depart from your house, because you despised me and took the wife of Uriah the Hittite to be your own' . . . . Then David said to Nathan, 'I have sinned against the Lord.' Nathan replied, 'The Lord has taken away your sin. You are not going to die. But because by doing this you have made the enemies of the Lord show utter contempt, the son born to you will die" (II Samuel 12:1-14).

Whenever a politician sins brazenly, take courage and draw inspiration from the prophet Nathan's example.

Because Americans mostly believe they're a special people, blessed with divine favor, and because of their "astonishing incapacity to understand why anyone should dislike [them] at all," sadly they are unable to conceive of Nemesis[47].

CHAPTER 3

A GODLY NATION . . . .

The annals of history teem with stories of evil deeds that, by means of invocation and rationalization, become transmogrified into noble and glorious exploits. Invoking nationalism or religious values or icons or necessity will end up transforming wickedness into righteousness, at least in the minds of some. And excusing the perpetrators through twisted and illogical argument turns spectators into accomplices. But the moral corruption doesn't stop there, for the onlooker busies herself with focusing on extraneous matters while not even paying attention to sins committed in her name. Lenin didn't patiently explain to the proletariat that the Bolshevik Revolution would entail copious bloodletting and deceptive propaganda unlike anything they'd ever seen under the Tsar. Instead he invoked *their* interests and dreams and called on them to unite as one behind him. Likewise, we in the US can't expect to escape divine punishment by either refusing to acknowledge and turn away from our past sins or invoking the Founding Fathers or the Pledge of Allegiance or patriotism or the Ten Commandments monument in Montgomery, Alabama.

The Lord rebuked the Israelites for the very same sin.

> "This is what the Lord Almighty, the God of Israel, says: Reform your ways and your actions, and I will let you live in this place. Do not trust in deceptive words and say, 'This is the temple of the Lord, the temple of the Lord, the temple of the Lord!' If you really change your ways and your actions and deal with each other justly, if you do not oppress the alien, the fatherless or the widow and do not shed innocent

blood in this place, and if you do not follow other gods to your own harm, then I will let you live in this place . . . . But look, you are trusting in deceptive words that are worthless. Will you steal and murder, commit adultery and perjury, . . . and follow other gods you have not known, and then come and stand before me in this house, which bears my Name, and say, 'We are safe'—safe to do all these detestable things? Has this house, which bears my Name, become a den of robbers to you? But I have been watching! declares the Lord . . . While you were doing all these things, declares the Lord, I spoke to you again and again, but you did not listen; I called you, but you did not answer . . . So do not pray for this people nor offer any plea or petition for them; do not plead with me, for I will not listen to you . . . But am I the one they are provoking? declares the Lord. Are they not rather harming themselves, to their own shame?'" (Jeremiah 7:3-11,13,16,19).

In 2001 "death has climbed in through our windows and has entered our fortresses" (Jeremiah 9:21). Will it do so again if God is against us?

Historian C. Gregg Singer wrote an interesting book detailing the theological milieu of our country since the arrival of the English colonists. Whereas the Pilgrims and the Puritans were clearly devout followers of Christ, in the intervening years before the American Revolution a sea change, a profound break with the past, occurred with the advent of Deism and the French Enlightenment. Prof. Singer says categorically:

> That the Jeffersonian democracy was founded on Christian principles and simply reflects the social implications of the Gospels is one of the . . . most persistent errors of contemporary America. The reference to God in the Declaration of Independence, and the apparent submission to his will, should not blind us to the tragic misuse of biblical ideas to convey Deistic principles for the realization of a society which would be essentially humanistic and anti-supernaturalistic in character"[48].

I would only add that Jefferson's language about submission to God's will, when juxtaposed with the robust and energetic war against the British authorities is, to put it charitably, rather ironic in light of the prohibition on armed rebellion in Romans 13 that we discussed in the first chapter. Would a Ugandan rebel militia that calls itself the Lord's Resistance Army and that recruits its members by kidnapping gain the approval of American Christians simply on the basis of its name?

To continue with Singer: historians Herbert Morais, John Orr and Richard Mosier have explicated the close philosophical connection between the American Revolution and Deism and the Enlightenment[49]. Philosopher Richard Popkin, in a more recent work, affirms this link. "Although there is still much debate about the [connections] between the French Enlightenment and the [French] revolution, many radical ideas of the *philosophes* became part of the revolutionary and postrevolutionary secular political worlds in Europe and America and have remained central ever since"[50].

A Godly Nation Doesn't Covet

Drawing mostly on American sources, British historian Robert Harvey has written a compelling and balanced history of the early years of our Republic called *'A Few Bloody Noses': The Realities and Mythologies of the American Revolution*[51]. Several of Harvey's ancestors were closely identified with British government policy toward the Americans. These include Prime Minister George Grenville, whose Stamp Act quickly achieved infamy among the revolutionaries across the pond, as well as William Pitt the Elder, a fervent opponent of British policy, and Thomas Grenville, one of the architects of the peace overtures that led to the Treaty of Paris.

Although they didn't emphasize this in their public pronouncements, a primary reason for rebelling against King George turns out to have been the Americans' "burning resentment at the British imposition of the Proclamation Line along the watershed of the Appalachians, beyond which land could not be settled by the whites at the expense of the large Indian population"[52].

"Thus the real spark for the American War of Independence
was to be the right of settlers to go on pushing westward at

the bloody expense of the Indians—which led to the decision to send in a British standing army and to tax the Americans to pay for it. Not surprisingly, American writers were later to prefer to concentrate on the taxation rather than the land grabs across the Appalachians as the catalyst of discontent; but the latter were the first link in the chain of causation"[53].

The colonists' indignation at taxation without representation "masked the true objection: that they were being asked to subsidize British troops blocking their westward expansion"[54]. But the very purpose for which God instituted government was to restrain evildoers. Recall the passage in Romans 13: He is God's servant, an agent of wrath to bring punishment on the wrongdoer (verse 4). "Grenville's policy was undoubtedly humane and respectful of moral rights and justice for the original inhabitants"[55].

A Godly Nation Doesn't Despise and Rebel Against Authority

In the century before the American Revolution, deists chipped away at the authority of church and state. Some of their writings even amounted to an ax placed at the roots of the *ancien regime*. According to Popkin,

> "the deist authors were engaged in a polemical and ideological war against a prevailing system of authority and cultural power represented by the *de jure divino* (divine right) institutions of church and state . . . . One of the key cultural foundations of the . . . early modern confessional state was the authority of the vernacular Bible. Authorized in 1611, the Bible was itself the religion of Protestants, a handbook not only of religious belief and practice, a guide to salvation and redemption, but also a text that reinforced and inscribed the structures of both social and political hierarchy. It is at this point that the frequently ignored connection between deism and politics is crucial. Rather than considering deists as a variety of radical Christian theologians, or as a point on some evolutionary vector in the history of ideas from Christian certainty to modern atheism, the deists are better seen as the first critics of cultural authority [per se] . . . . [T]he assault was achieved by concentrating on the key texts of scripture

and revelation . . . . The point of much deistic writing was not just to challenge specific Christian . . . beliefs . . ., but to suggest that the very notion of establishing a conformity in articles of belief was corrupt . . . . [A]n arch proponent of the . . . critique of the Bible was John Toland [(1670-1722)] . . . . [H]e published the first significant moves against the authenticity of the Bible . . . . Much of the intellectual work that underpinned the high Enlightenment's attack upon [orthodoxy] had been mapped out by the English deists. Thomas Paine's *Age of Reason* (1794-1795)—often characterized as the epitome of Enlightenment irreligion—far from being an innovative assault on Christian mystery and the authority of the Bible, drew many of its arguments from the earlier deistic writings"[56].

The Apostle Peter writes eloquently and at some length about unrighteous men who "follow the corrupt desire of the sinful nature and despise authority" (II Peter 2:10ff). "For our offenses are many in your sight . . . : turning our backs on our God, fomenting oppression and revolt" (Isaiah 59:12,13). "Fear the Lord and the king, my son, and do not join with the rebellious" (Proverbs 24:21). "Remind the people to be subject to rulers and authorities, to be obedient . . . to slander no one, to be peaceable and considerate, and to show true humility toward all men" (Titus 3:1-2). But our forefathers reacted so violently to passage of the Stamp Act that British officials were driven out of town. "[I]n Rhode Island the collector of the customs and the distributors of the stamps [were] obliged to take refuge on board a ship"[57]. In Boston the lieutenant-governor's furniture was chopped into pieces and his money stolen by rioting American home invaders[58]. But rather than decry the rebellion against Britain, we Christians celebrate it. "Thus you nullify the word of God for the sake of your tradition" (Matthew 15:6).

A Godly Nation Doesn't Use God as a Stalking Horse

Again we refer to the analysis of Prof. Singer:

> "This Jeffersonian democracy rested on the denial of the sovereignty of God [in the sense that] Jeffersonians, as Boorstin

has observed, 'put God at the service of their earthly American task.' A creator, God had abdicated his throne to his creation, and his role was to be one of cooperating with men in the realization of the American Dream"[59].

In an antique store someone chanced upon a statue of an American Indian god with enormous ears and a tiny mouth. Our forefathers would've approved of this kind of god.

John Bunyan's *Pilgrim's Progress* has much to say on this matter:

> "For if it be unlawful to follow Christ for loaves (as it is in John 6:26), how much more abominable is it to make of Him and religion a stalking-horse to get and enjoy the world! Nor do we find any other than heathens, hypocrites, devils and witches, that are of this opinion.
>
> 1.) Heathens: for when Hamor and Shechem had a mind to the daughters and cattle of Jacob, and saw that there was no way for them to come at them but by being circumcised, they say to their companions, 'If every male of us be circumcised, as they are circumcised, shall not their cattle and their substance, and every beast of theirs, be ours?' Their daughters and their cattle were that which they sought to obtain, and their religion the stalking-horse they made use of to come at them. Read the whole story. (Genesis 34:20-24).
>
> 2.) The hypocritical Pharisees were also of this religion: long prayers were their pretence; but to get widows' houses was their intent, and greater damnation was from God their judgment (Luke 20:46-47).
>
> 3.) Judas, the devil, was also of this religion: he was religious for the bag, that he might be possessed of what was put therein; but he was lost, cast away, and the very son of perdition.

4.) Simon, the wizard, was of this religion too: for he would have had the Holy Ghost, that he might have got money therewith; and his sentence from Peter's mouth was according (Acts 8:18-23).

5.) Neither will it go out of my mind, but that that man who takes up religion for the world, will throw away religion for the world; for so surely as Judas designed the world in becoming religious, so surely did he also sell religion and his Master for the same."

Although it's true that the Protestant anti-Establishment churches supported the Revolution, "the radicals manipulated the Protestants and their ethics for their own ends rather than the other way around"[60].

"How can you say, 'We are wise, for we have the law of the Lord,' when actually the lying pen of the scribes has handled it falsely?" (Jeremiah 8:8). A pastor named Dr. Mayhew even incited his flock to violence during the riots in Boston that followed the Stamp Act. "[He] preached on a text out of the Galatians, 'I would they were cut off which trouble you: for, brethren, ye are called unto liberty,' and in his sermon inveighed with the utmost vehemence of expression and gesture against the Stamp Act, which . . . so irritated his heated audience, that it was with difficulty they were restrained by the observance of the Sabbath, and the next day burst forth into . . . violence"[61].

Or Ethnically Cleanse

Was the forcible and merciless removal of the First Americans from their ancient homeland by the latecomers an unfortunate consequence of rank and file soldiers taking matters into their own hands? No, rather

"[t]he decision to carry the war into Indian territory on a large scale, to pursue scorched earth tactics, to give no quarter to the fighters, to destroy hundreds of settlements, and to starve the women and children in a deliberate effort to expel them from a great swath of their own territory was . . . the stated policy of both Washington and Congress . . . [I]t for ever besmirches the reputations of the founding fathers who ordered it . . . The destruction of extensive settlements covering so large an area of territory was in fact a methodical cleansing of the land of its inhabitants, as a result of that relentless pressure for colonization of tribal lands which had triggered Indian hostility to the American settlers in the first place"[62].

Thus were the sins of coveting, stealing and murdering combined into one evil from which the descendants of these savages avert their gaze while intoning—without a trace of irony—the mantra of our Judeo-Christian heritage. Alas, no department of homeland security could save their victims from the onslaught of overwhelming pitiless brute force. "On your clothes men find the lifeblood of the innocent poor, though you did not catch them breaking in. Yet in spite of all this you say 'I am innocent; he is not angry with me.' But I will pass judgment on you because you say 'I have not sinned'" (Jeremiah 2:34-35). "Yet you have the brazen look of a prostitute; you refuse to blush with shame. Have you not just called to me: 'My Father, my friend from my youth, will you always be angry? Will your wrath continue forever?' This is how you talk, but you do all the evil you can" (Jeremiah 3:3-5).

The sequel to this wickedness is better known. In 1815, unarable land west of the Mississippi River was formally established as Indian Country. President Madison advocated relocation of all eastern tribes. Congress helpfully passed the Indian Removal Act of 1830 to move all of the First Americans to the West[63].

"The wise will be put to shame; they will be dismayed and trapped. Since they have rejected the word of the Lord, what kind of wisdom do they have? . . . From the least to the greatest, all are greedy for gain; prophets and priests alike, all practice deceit . . . . Are they ashamed of their loathsome conduct? No, they have no shame at all; they do not even know how to blush. So they will fall among the fallen; they will be brought down when they are punished,' says the Lord" (Jeremiah 8:9,10,12).

Or Massacre

Robert Harvey writes of the little-known frontier war between the whites and Indians:

> "Once war broke out between the British and the Americans, from north to south along the western border a no-holds-barred systematic holocaust was carried out against the Indian tribes . . .—largely by militia raised from among the land-hungry white border settlers with the full support of Washington and the American high command. This was devastatingly successful, and opened the way to the full-scale occupation of Indian lands during the following century. Thousands of Indians were massacred in the process . . . and probably tens of thousands of Indians deliberately starved to death . . . ."[64].

Not content with this savagery, the Americans even massacred non-hostile Christian Indians. According to an eyewitness account, a missionary named David Zeisberger led about a hundred converted Delawares to their home village of Gnadenhutten where they welcomed some Pennsylvania militia. "The militia promptly took the pro-American Delawares prisoner, occupied the old Moravian schoolhouse in the village, and had the prisoners brought in one by one to be bludgeoned to death—supposedly to save the trouble of taking the prisoners back to Fort Pitt"[65].

In 1864, a Cheyenne chief named Black Kettle went to Sand Creek to sue for peace. "While he and his warriors were out hunting, those who remained in the camp—mostly women and children—were the victims of a vicious massacre by white volunteers"[66]. "In East Saint Louis, Illinois [in 1917], at least 200 African Americans die[d] in a race riot and hundreds [were] injured." In 1943, "close to 275 race riots [broke] out in some 50 cities, including Detroit and New York City's Harlem"[67].

The pilgrim Christian in John Bunyan's tale encountered great hostility from the inhabitants of the town Vanity Fair because he put so little store by their merchandise, namely

> "houses, lands, trades, places, honours, preferments, titles, countries, kingdoms, lusts, pleasures; and delights of all sorts—as harlots, wives, husbands, children, masters, servants, lives, blood, bodies, souls, silver, gold, pearls, precious stones, and what not. And, moreover, at this fair there are at all times to be seen jugglings, cheats, games, plays, fools, apes, knaves, and rogues, and that of every kind. Here are to be seen, too, and that for nothing, thefts, murders, adulteries, false-swearers, and that of a blood-red colour."

Christian and his fellow pilgrims were asked by a merchant what they wished to buy, whereupon they responded "We buy the truth" (Proverbs 23:23). Would our Founding Fathers feel out of place in Vanity Fair or, rather, right at home? And how would they have reacted to multinational forces bent on regime change here due to our ferocious repression of minorities?

Or Lynch

Charles Lynch was a Virginia justice of the peace whose gruesome—not to mention extralegal—way of dispatching Tories during the Revolution was named after him. Already by the end of the 1700s this barbarous crime had become an American tradition. Between 1880 and 1930 "a black person was murdered by a white mob nearly every week"[68]. The tally of lynched African Americans had exceeded 3,500 by the 1960s. Journalist Ida Wells Barnett investigated the causes of the deed and determined that rape or attempted rape were usually not a factor[69]. Besides, David Levering Lewis writes that the number of white men who raped black women with impunity far surpassed black on white rape[70]. Ms Barnett concluded that lynching victims were mostly murdered for outspokenness in order to "frighten and intimidate African Americans both politically and socially"[71]. Dare we call this terrorism and the perps terrorists? Do some among us secretly harbor even to this day a laughable belief in white superiority? Well then, please note that among *your* favored race were "souvenir hunters [who] would fight over severed testicles and strips of barbecued flesh"[72].

Or Murder Innocents in War

A Native American chief of the Onondaga tribe described an attack on his village by supposedly civilized whites during the Revolutionary War: "They put to death all the women and children, excepting some of the young women, whom they carried away for the use of their soldiers and were afterwards put to death in a more shameful manner"[73]. Isaiah laments that "whoever shuns evil becomes a prey" (Isaiah 59:15) and, sadly, that was true of pro-British citizens. "Several Quakers, guilty of no more than non-belligerence, were in fact publicly hanged, and others were imprisoned and fined by the courts"[74].

And among many 20th-century examples of this sin, one particularly heinous instance occurred on March 10, 1945 when we dropped napalm on Tokyo, taking at least 80,000 lives in a single night.

Or Act Brutally

Col. George Rogers Clark believed that "to exceed them in barbarity was, and is, the only way to make war upon Indians and gain a name among them." He put shoe leather on this repellent thought when he ambushed some Indians heading back to their lodgings "and personally led his men in tomahawking them"[75]. "William Henry Drayton and Andrew Williamson of South Carolina advocated that captured Indians should become the slaves of the captors, but the legislature refused, fearing Indian retaliation for such a precedent. Since Indian prisoners brought no reward, soldiers killed them for their scalps." Both South Carolina and Pennsylvania offered cash for Indian scalps. "Kentucky militiamen who invaded Shawnee villages dug up graves to scalp corpses"[76]. Even British soldiers were scalped. One, found dying by fellow troops, had "had his brain and ears removed with a hatchet"[77].

"The Pennsylvania legislature passed a brutal measure providing extreme penalties for certain specified severe offences of helping the enemy, whereby estates could be forfeited and imprisonment imposed for 'treason, including every or any resistance to the government, stirring up tumults or opposing revolutionary acts.' No fewer that 500 people were stripped of their property in Pennsylvania alone"[78].

And a century later, "the evidence of race conflict and violence, brutality and exploitation in this . . . period is overwhelming"[79]. The reason for the triumph of these evildoers was "a general weakening and discrediting of the numerous forces that had hitherto kept them in check, [including] not only Northern liberal opinion in the press, the courts, and the government, but also internal checks imposed by the prestige and influence of the Southern conservatives, as well as by the idealism and zeal of the Southern radicals." The waning of Northern resistance to oppression partly stemmed from a sincere desire for sectional reconciliation. Ironically, "just as the [African American] gained his emancipation and new rights through a falling out between white men, he now stood to lose his rights through the reconciliation of white men"[80].

Or Terrorize

The Ku Klux Klan reached its zenith of 4 million or more members in the mid-1920s, expanded into the North and Midwest, and terrorized not only blacks but immigrants, Catholics and Jews[81].

Or Mistreat Fugitive Slaves

Every American schoolkid learns about Abraham Lincoln's Emancipation Proclamation, but the loyalist governor of Virginia, Lord Dunmore, issued one, too. In November 1775 he declared "all indentured servants, negroes, or others (appertaining to rebels), free, that are able and willing to bear arms, they joining His Majesty's troops, as soon as may be, for the more speedily reducing the colony to a proper sense of their duty, to His Majesty's crown and dignity." As a result, slaveowners were seriously alarmed and enraged. Washington thought that "if that man [Dunmore] is not crushed before spring, he will become the most formidable enemy America has"[82]. Dire warnings were issued threatening death without benefit of clergy to slaves who rose up in insurrection. Some hapless recaptured runaways did in fact meet an untimely end at the hands of their masters[83].

A similar proclamation, this one by the British commander-in-chief Sir Henry Clinton on June 30, 1779 (one wonders why he didn't delay until the 4th of July) caused swarms of blacks to cross over to the British side. American retaliation was brutal. "One well-known black river pilot, 'Jerry,' caught assisting slaves to flee to the British in South Carolina . . . was hanged and his body burnt . . . . The loyalist governor protested [that] 'the very act harrows my soul,' but the local assembly threatened to carry out the sentence outside his mansion. In 1776 the state imposed the death penalty on any slave joining or supporting the British, and executions were frequently carried out. Virginia did the same, but applied the noose more sparingly. Other, more lenient, states would sell offending slaves who were caught to new owners abroad"[84].

But God says that "if a slave has taken refuge with you, do not hand him over to his master. Let him live among you wherever he likes and in whatever town he chooses. Do not oppress him" (Deuteronomy 23:15-16). Our forebears could've done more to accommodate this command.

Or Kidnap

As manpower shortages grew worse and worse in the American army, able-bodied African Americans were simply kidnapped ('press-ganged') into the service[85].

Just a few short years after the adoption of the Constitution, Congress passed the Fugitive Slave Act of 1793, which exposed free Northern blacks to the grave danger of "enslavement through kidnapping or mistaken identity"[86].

As the reader can well imagine, God's attitude is somewhat different. "Anyone who kidnaps another and either sells him or still has him when he is caught must be put to death" (Exodus 21:16).

Or Trade Slaves

"We know that the law is good if a man uses it properly. We also know that law is made not for good men but for lawbreakers and rebels, the ungodly and sinful, the unholy and irreligious; for those who kill their fathers or mothers, for murderers, for adulterers and perverts, for slave traders and liars and perjurers . . . ." (I Timothy 1:8-10).

Or Embrace Injustice

Congress changed the 1793 Fugitive Slave Act in 1850, making it harsher and more arbitrary. Now

> "accused fugitives could not testify on their own behalf or benefit from trial by jury. [Also, law enforcement officials] received five dollars if they decided that the black person before them was not a slave but were paid ten dollars if they [decided the contrary]. In Christiana [Penn.] more than forty men were indicted for treason [!!] after a group of fugitives fought their would-be captors and killed a slaveowner. [They] were released when U.S. Supreme Court Justice Robert Grier, on circuit, ruled in *United States v. Hanway* (1851) that opposition to the Fugitive Slave Act did not constitute treason"[87].

An op-ed piece in *The Economist*, a British newsmagazine, condemned Pres. Bush's military commissions in sweeping terms.

> The regulations explicitly deny [the defendant] any enforceable rights of the sort that criminal defendants won as long ago as the Middle Ages. Moreover, the . . . commissions lack the one element indispensable to any genuinely fair proceeding—an independent judiciary, both for the trial itself and for any appeal against a conviction. The military officers sitting as judges belong to a single chain of command reporting to the secretary of defense and the president, who will designate any accused for trial before the commissions

and will also hear any final appeals. For years, America has rightly condemned the use of similar military courts in other countries for denying due process"[88].

Arthur Schlesinger Jr wrote an impassioned letter to *The New York Review of Books* which should disturb conservatives, for they above all others have zealously defended the idea of limited government circumscribed by constitutional safeguards:

> The situation of the detainees at Guantánamo is a national disgrace. [They] have been imprisoned for two years. They are ignorant of the specific charges against them and denied access to legal counsel and to their families. Although five British prisoners have been released, a 'senior defense official' tells *The New York Times* that other detainees will be held for many years, perhaps indefinitely. Some among them have attempted suicide.
>
> It is difficult to find serious security reasons for the presidential suspension of due process. It appears to be, once again, the politics of fear and the imperial presidency redux. We have been through paranoid phases before, succumbing to panic and forgetting our constitutional guarantees. It all began in 1798 with the Alien and Sedition Acts. The Federalists would have been better advised to call these obnoxious statutes the Patriot Acts, but the conservatives of 1798 were innocent of the fine art of public relations.
>
> Recovering from our periodic attacks of panic, we have always hated ourselves in the morning. A generation from now the case of the Guantánamo detainees will be regarded as a national shame"[89].

Indeed James Madison sharply criticized the Alien and Sedition acts. He implored his fellow citizens to guard against 'executive aggrandizement' of which 'war is in fact the true nurse.' In his "Report of 1800" he wrote of these Acts that "all the principles 'of the only preventive justice known to American jurisprudence, are violated . . .'" and that they "would be likely to repress 'information and communication among the people,' and eventually to 'destroy our free system of government'"[90]. Elsewhere he wrote that "'the fetters imposed on liberty at home have ever been forged out of the weapons provided for defense against real, pretended, or imaginary dangers from abroad' . . . Madison wrote of the United States (and France) in 1799 [that] 'The propagation and management of alarms has grown into a kind of system [and] the people [are] more firm and enlightened than ought to be expected, if they are not in some measure awed or duped into a tacit acquiescence under oppression'"[91].

"In the Tryal of Persons accused for Crimes against the State, the Method is much more short and commendable: The Judge first sends to sound the Disposition of those in Power; after which he can easily hang or save the Criminal, strictly preserving all the Forms of Law"[92]. The essence of tyranny is unbridled, unaccountable caprice.

"Cursed is the man who withholds justice from the alien, the fatherless or the widow" (Deuteronomy 27:19).

In October 2002, Brett Bursey was arrested at a Columbia, South Carolina airport while holding a sign reading 'No War for Oil.' Federal charges were brought against him the following March under an obscure law which, prosecutors say, restricts protestors to a designated 'free-speech zone' which, in this case, was half a mile from where the President was to give a speech. The penalty in the event of a conviction would be 6 months in jail and a $5,000 fine. But Mr Bursey pointed out to arresting officers that all of America was designated a free-speech zone[93].

Or Oppress

Chief Joseph of the Nez Perce tribe naturally wished to avoid having his people forced onto a reservation. So he led them on a 1,500-mile trek through three northwestern states under war conditions with the Americans in pursuit. When the former were finally defeated, they were put on a reservation[94].

The Supreme Court aided the oppressors by ruling in Lone Wolf v. Hitchcock (1903) that "tribal lands were [not] taken without due process." The Court "also foreclose[d] any avenue of appeal on grounds that Indians are wards of the federal government and thus cannot sue their own guardian"[95]. Are they 'children'?!?!

And what can be said about refusing to educate slaves? One early Puritan

> "long lamented . . . with a bleeding and a burning passion, that the [whites] used their [slaves] but as their horses or their oxen, and that so little care was taken about their immortal souls; he looked upon it as a [shame] that any wearing the name of Christians, should so much have the heart of devils in them, as to prevent and hinder [their] instruction . . . and confine [their] souls . . . to a destroying ignorance, merely for fear of thereby losing the benefit of their [labor]"[96].

The state of California weighed in with several oppressive measures, too. Its 1879 constitution kept Chinese jobseekers out of the labor force altogether. Also the 1913 Alien Land Law and a 1920 law prohibited Japanese from owning any property or leasing farmland in the state[97].

And then there's the infamous imprisonment of Japanese-American citizens in concentration camps by Franklin Roosevelt merely because of their ethnic origin. They lost about $400 million in property as a result[98].

"Blessed is he whose help is the God of Jacob, whose hope is in the Lord his God, the Maker of heaven and earth, the sea, and everything in them— the Lord, who remains faithful forever. He upholds the cause of the oppressed" (Psalm 146:5-7).

Or Hate Races Perpetually

Were it possible to imagine such a thing, suppose Canadians came pouring across the border every spring to rape, pillage and plunder.

Then suppose we were dragged kicking and screaming to Canada and forced to perform menial tasks like starting their cars on winter mornings, thawing out car door handles and deicing windshields and other glass surfaces, not to mention shoveling mountains of snow. After a few years of freezing our buns off up north, it wouldn't be surprising if feelings of resentment and hatred toward Canadians began to boil up inside us. Now imagine our response if *they* hated and resented *us*, their victims. Does this make any sense at all? Well no, of course not, but this is how African Americans have been treated for centuries.

> For arrogance and hatred are the wares
> Peddled in the thoroughfares.
> Yeats, "A Prayer for My Daughter"

This vice knows no sectional boundaries either. Indeed "[o]ne of the strangest things about [segregation] was that the system was born in the North and reached an advanced age before moving South in force." And Alexis de Tocqueville was astonished by the intensity of Northern racism. "'The prejudice of race,' he wrote, 'appears to be stronger in the states that have abolished slavery than in those where it still exists; and nowhere is it so intolerant as in those states where servitude has never been known'"[99].

Or Destroy Private Property

In the frontier war alluded to earlier, in a manner harking back to, and with a ferocity worthy of, Attila the Hun, the Americans burned down hundreds of Indian villages and destroyed thousands of tons of crops[100]. During one of these raids,

> "in 1779, Chicamauga Cherokee country was invaded . . . and eleven villages as well as 20,000 bushels of corn were destroyed and £25,000 worth of goods seized . . .
>
> All this was no more than official policy. Congress had decreed that 'no mercy' was to be shown to 'those that have been at war against the States.' Washington, in respect of the Iroquois

expedition into the Mohawk and Susquehanna valleys, had ordered that his men should act 'To carry the war into the heart of the [Indian] Six Nations; to cut off their settlements, destroy their next year's crops, and do them every other mischief of which time and circumstances will permit . . . it will be essential to ruin their crops now in the ground and prevent them planting more.' Even the 'liberal' Jefferson had called for the Shawnees to be driven from their land or exterminated"[101].

And we all know about the Boston Tea Party, when criminals dumped 45 tons of tea overboard[102]. In what sense was this act of vandalism a 'party'?

Or Steal

The seizure of Indian territory has already been related in graphic detail. Not content with this, the whites also commandeered the commerce that crossed the Appalachian mountains, including a lucrative fur trade[103]. "In addition, the importance of the American colonies' thriving trade in piracy and smuggling cannot be overstated. Raiding Spanish ships was estimated to bring £100,000 a year to New York alone . . . At least £1 million a year flowed into North America from piracy compared with £40,000 a year taken in British tax revenues from the colonies"[104]. And what student of US history hasn't heard the infamous slogan 'manifest destiny,' coined in 1845 by a journalist named John O'Sullivan, to warm the hearts of thieves with western lands in their sights[105]?

Or Bully

In 1768, the political extremist Samuel Adams "used intimidation freely, resorting to violence through brawny lieutenants when necessary, and literally forced the merchants of Boston to disobey the law, regardless of their own wishes, loyalty to the Crown or desire to earn a living as they saw fit"[106]. When loyalist Governor Thomas Hutchinson decided he'd have nothing to do with a growing boycott of British imports, a mob showed up and "threaten[ed] to tear down his warehouse until he caved in." In another case, a businessman named Theophilus Lillie heeded the boycott but protested how strange it was that

> "men who are guarding against being subject to laws [to] which they never gave their consent in person or by their representative, should at the same time make laws, and in the most effectual manner execute them upon me and others, to which laws I am sure I never gave my consent either in person or by my representative . . . I had rather be a slave under one master; for if I know who he is, I may, perhaps, be able to please him, than a slave to a hundred or more, who I don't know where to find, nor what they will expect of me."

The mob responded to this eloquent yet fruitless appeal by nailing an 'informer' sign over his shop. "[I]n the fracas that followed, an eleven-year-old boy was killed"[107].

British Gen. Thomas Gage grew to detest the citizens of Boston. "America," he said, "is a mere bully, from one end to the other, and the Bostonians by far the greatest bullies." One of his subordinates, Lord Percy, echoed this view of the latter, describing them as "a set of sly, artful, hypocritical rascals, cruel and cowards"[108]. The bullies made a mockery of freedom of the press by terrorizing the *Boston News Letter* into submission[109].

"From a very early stage the [revolutionaries] understood the need to force ordinary people to support the American cause; their network of coercion vastly outstripped anything the British could muster"[110].

Does Pay Taxes

Propagandists for the American side would have us believe that the King's tax regime was unbearably burdensome, but actually taxes and customs duties were lower than in Britain itself, and "almost entirely unenforced, the great bulk of America's trade being contraband." Our coastline was a "smuggling haven"[111]. We even became enraged when Parliament passed a new tax, the famous Stamp Act.

"'Is it right for us to pay taxes to Caesar or not?' [Jesus] saw through their duplicity and said to them, 'Show me a [coin]. Whose portrait and inscription are on it?' 'Caesar's' they replied. He said to them, 'Then give to Caesar what is Caesar's, and to God what is God's'" (Luke 20:22-25).

Doesn't Act Treacherously

After the Battle of Saratoga the Americans betrayed a promise to allow the British troops safe passage home[112]. And the Northwest Ordinance of 1787 promised that "the utmost good faith shall always be observed towards the Indians; their lands and property shall never be taken from them without their consent"[113].

Isn't Hypocritical

Jupiter Hammon wrote these poignant words in 1787:

> "That liberty is a great thing we know from our own feelings, and we may likewise judge so from the conduct of the white people in the late war. How much money has been spent and how many lives have been lost to defend their liberty! I must say that I have hoped that God would open their eyes, when they were so much engaged for liberty, to think of the state of the poor blacks, and to pity us."

Mr Hammon remained in bondage throughout his life[114].

"Blessed is he who has regard for the weak; the Lord delivers him in times of trouble" (Psalm 41:1). "Do to others as you would have them do to you. Be merciful, just as your Father is merciful" (Luke 6:31,36). The hypocritical reaction of the slavemasters to Sir Henry Clinton's emancipation proclamation of 1779 has already been noted. Among our southern Founding Fathers, the only honorable response was that of James Madison. "He said he was unable to [punish his slave Billy] 'merely for coveting that liberty for which we had paid the price of so much blood, and have proclaimed so often to be the right, and worthy pursuit of every human being.' Billy was sent to Pennsylvania as an indentured servant, and was freed after seven years"[115].

In a letter to the British government, Prime Minister Grenville's chief adviser on American affairs, Thomas Whately, complained after white murderers of Cherokees were rescued from the clutches of the authorities by fellow whites that "these people seem to profess that killing an Indian is not a civil offence"[116].

Untold numbers of slave women were raped with impunity by their masters who, although they got away with it in human terms, must still face their Creator on the Day of Judgment. But all a black man had to do was make a suggestive remark or leer at a white woman (or someone could simply falsely claim that he did so) and chances were a baying lynch mob would snuff out his young life in a matter of hours[117].

The detestable sin of hypocrisy likewise found a home in the hearts of those who were determined to reconstruct the defeated South in light of a standard not yet widely embraced in the North. "It is clear," C. Vann Woodward writes, "that when . . . the time came, the North was not in the best possible position to instruct the South, either by precedent and example, or by force of conviction, on the implementation of what eventually became one of the professed war aims of the Union cause— racial equality"[118].

The 1940 Smith Act prohibits calling for armed revolution against our own government[119], although precisely the same method was employed to found it.

And have those who demand regime change these days considered the rage we'd feel (except our victims) were *our* homeland whacked for its ferocious treatment of certain ethnic groups? Can you imagine Teddy

Roosevelt getting bumped off by invading Chinese bound and determined to conquer and re-engineer our social and political institutions because we don't meet their high moral standards? And wait till our armed resisters are branded 'thugs' and 'death squads'!

Doesn't Let The End Justify The Means

If all human life is sacred, if every person is made in God's image in terms of knowledge, righteousness and holiness, then murdering abortion doctors is every bit as wicked as murdering others. To advance a career through hard work and study or to experience anger at a man for an unwanted pregnancy are both understandable, but sacrificing an innocent child to attain financial success or wreak revenge is still wrong. Likewise with using murder, torture or deceit to achieve political objectives.

On issues like setting up the Department of Homeland Security, our nation's attitude toward the UN, steel tariffs, intelligence about the missing WMD, biometric security measures at US airports and a host of others, the Bush White House approach was bereft of principle. Is the President *against* a Homeland Security Dept.? At first yes, but now he's *for* it. Are we the sheriff to Mayor Kofi Annan's resolution 1441? Or is the UN just a bunch of fraudulent multilateralists? Or is Annan our guiding light on the transition process to Iraqi self-rule? Are we dead set against Shiite dominance of Iraq? But the Administration caved in just a few hours after Grand Ayatollah Sistani expressed mild displeasure about its proposed election caucuses. Are we in favor of free trade? But a steel tariff might sway voters in certain swing states. Can't get solid intel on those 'quantum' WMD (when one looks at them, they vanish)? No sweat, we'll set up an Office of Special Plans to stovepipe unverified defector claims straight up to Defense Secretary Rumsfeld himself. But when Hussein Kamal, son-in-law to Saddam Hussein, defects in 1995 and insists that those weapons have already been destroyed, the stovepipe gets bent temporarily to allow the business end to point at a trash can. "This willingness to abandon principles in the blind desire to produce results is becoming a theme of the Bush presidency"[120].

Does Live Peaceably

John Bunyan vividly describes the verbal and physical abuse suffered by the pilgrims at the hands of Vanity Fair's denizens. These harmless souls were beaten and smeared with dirt and made a spectacle of in a cage. The locals made fun of them and took malicious action for the 'sin' of not caring for their merchandise. Nevertheless, Christian and Faithful bore it all patiently,

> "not rendering railing for railing, but, contrariwise, blessing, and giving good words for bad, and kindness for injuries done, [so that] some men in the fair that were more observing and less prejudiced than the rest, began to check and blame the baser sort for their continual abuses done by them to the men. They, therefore, in angry manner, let fly at them again, counting them as bad as the men in the cage, and telling them that they seemed confederates, and should be made partakers of their misfortunes. The others replied, that for aught they could see, the men were quiet and sober, and intended nobody any harm; and that there were many that traded in their fair that were more worthy to be put into the cage, yea, and pillory too, than were the men that they had abused."

Does Stand For Righteousness Even Against Strong Opposition

As Christian continues on his pilgrimage, accompanied by Hopeful—alas, Faithful has been executed in Vanity Fair by this time—they meet a traveler called By-Ends, a nickname given to him because "I had always the luck to [agree] in my judgment with the present way of the times, whatever it was, and my chance was to get [something] thereby." Yet Christian was not the kind to go with the flow. Those who follow Jesus,

> "after their headstrong manner [so says By-Ends], conclude that it is their duty to rush on their journey all weathers; and I am for waiting for wind and tide. They are for hazarding all

for God at a clap; and I am for taking all advantages to secure my life and estate. They are for holding their notions, though all other men be against them; but I am for religion in what, and so far as, the times and my safety will bear it. They are for Religion when in rags and contempt; but I am for him when he walks in his silver slippers, in the sunshine, and with applause."

Isn't Self-righteous

"To some who were confident of their own righteousness and looked down on everybody else, Jesus told this parable: 'Two men went up to the temple to pray, one a Pharisee and the other a tax collector. The Pharisee stood up and prayed about himself; 'God, I thank you that I am not like all other men—robbers, evildoers, adulterers—or even like this tax collector. I fast twice a week and give a tenth of all I get.'

But the tax collector stood at a distance. He would not even look up to heaven, but beat his breast and said, 'God, have mercy on me, a sinner.'

I tell you that this man, rather than the other, went home justified before God. For everyone who exalts himself will be humbled, and he who humbles himself will be exalted'" (Luke 18:9-14).

Doesn't Refuse to Repent of Sin

"Now, said Christian, let me go hence. Nay, stay, said the Interpreter, till I have showed thee a little more, and after that thou shalt go thy way. So he took him by the hand again, and led him into a very dark room, where there sat a man in an iron cage.

Now the man, to look on, seemed very sad: he sat with his eyes looking down to the ground, his hands folded together, and he sighed as if he would break his heart. Then said Christian, What means this? At which the Interpreter bid him talk with the man.

Then said Christian to the man, What art thou? The man answered, I am what I was not once.

CHRISTIAN. What was thou once?

MAN. The man said, I was once a fair and flourishing professor [ie, a nominal Christian], both in mine own eyes and also in the eyes of others. I was once, as I thought, fair for the Celestial City, and had even joy at the thoughts that I should get thither . . .

CHRISTIAN. Well, but what art thou now?

MAN. I am now a man of despair, and am shut up in it, as in this iron cage. I cannot get out; oh, now I cannot!

CHRISTIAN. But how camest thou into this condition?

MAN. I left off to watch and be sober; I laid the reins upon the neck of my lusts; I sinned against the light of the World and the goodness of God. I have grieved the Spirit, and he is gone; I tempted the devil, and he is come to me; I have provoked God to anger, and he has left me. I have so hardened my heart, that I cannot repent.

Then said Christian to the Interpreter, But are there no hopes for such a man as this? Ask him, said the Interpreter.

CHRISTIAN. Then said Christian, Is there no hope, but you must be kept in the iron cage of despair?

MAN. No, none at all.

CHRISTIAN. Why, the Son of the Blessed is very [merciful].

MAN. I have crucified Him to myself afresh. I have despised His person; I have despised His righteousness; I have counted His blood an unholy thing; I have done despite to the Spirit of grace . . . therefore, I have shut myself out of all the promises, and there now remains to me nothing but threatenings, dreadful threatenings, fearful threatenings of certain judgment and fiery indignation, which shall devour me as an adversary.

CHRISTIAN. For what did you bring yourself into this condition?

MAN. For the lusts, pleasures, and profits of this world; in the enjoyment of which I did then promise myself much delight: but now every one of those things also bite me, and gnaw me like a burning worm.

CHRISTIAN. But canst thou not now repent and turn?

MAN. God hath denied me repentance. His Word gives me no encouragement to believe; yea, He himself hath shut me up in this iron cage: nor can all men in the world let me out. O eternity! eternity! how shall I grapple with the misery that I must meet with in eternity?

INTERPRETER. Then said the Interpreter to Christian, Let this man's misery be remembered by thee, and be an everlasting caution to thee.

CHRISTIAN. Well, said Christian. this is fearful! God help me to watch and be sober, and to pray that I may shun the cause of this man's misery."

And yet our forefathers were not only intent on pursuing evil, as this chapter makes abundantly clear, but they also were guilty of "the crowning offense of applauding those who practiced wickedness in its various manifestations. Instead of repenting of their own misdeeds and seeking to deter others, they promoted wrongdoing by encouraging it in their fellows, allying themselves with wanton sinners in defiant revolt against a righteous God"[121]. "Although they know God's righteous decree that those who do such things deserve death, they not only continue to do these very things but also approve of those who practice them" (Romans 1:32).

A Godly Nation Does God's Will

CHRISTIAN. This man, with whom you are so taken, will beguile with this tongue of his twenty of them that know him not . . . His name is Talkative . . . and, notwithstanding his fine tongue, he is but a sorry fellow . . . Religion hath no place in his heart, or house, or [conduct]; all he hath is in his tongue, and his religion is to make a noise therewith.

FAITHFUL. Say you so? Then am I in this man greatly deceived.

CHRISTIAN. Deceived! you may be sure of it. Remember the proverb 'they do not practice what they preach' (Matthew 23:3) but the 'kingdom of God is not a matter of talk but of power' (I Corinthians 4:20). He talketh of prayer, of repentance, of faith, and of the new birth; but he knows but only to talk of them. I have been in his family, and have observed him both at home and abroad; and I know what I say of him is the truth. His house is as empty of religion as the white of an egg is of savour. There is there neither prayer, nor sign of repentance for sin; yea, the brute, in his kind, serves God far better than he. He is the very stain, reproach, and shame of religion, to all that know him . . . it can hardly have a good word in all that end of the town where he dwells, through him . . . Besides, he brings up his sons to follow his steps; and if he finds in any of them a foolish timorousness (for so he calls the first appearance of a tender conscience), he calls them fools and blockheads, and by no means will employ them in much, or speak to their commendation before others. For my part, I am of opinion that he has, by his wicked life, caused many to stumble and fall; and will be, if God prevents not, the ruin of many more . . . Besides, good men are ashamed of him; they can neither call him brother nor friend; the very naming of him among them makes them blush, if they know him . . . he thinks that hearing and saying will make a good Christian; and thus he deceiveth his own soul. Hearing is but as the sowing of the seed; talking is not sufficient to prove that fruit is indeed in the heart and life. And let us assure ourselves, that at the day of doom, men shall be judged according to their fruits . . . It will not be said then, Did you believe? but, Were you doers, or talkers only? and accordingly shall they be judged. The end of the world is compared to our harvest . . . and you know, men at harvest regard nothing but fruit. Not that anything can be accepted that is not of faith; but I speak this to show you how insignificant the profession of Talkative will be at that day . . .

FAITHFUL. Well, I was not so fond of his company at first, but I am sick of it now. What shall we do to be rid of him?

CHRISTIAN. Take my advice, and do as I bid you, and you shall find that he will soon be sick of your company too, except God shall touch his heart and turn it.

FAITHFUL. What would you have me to do?

CHRISTIAN. Why, go to him, and enter into some serious discourse about the 'power' of religion; and ask him plainly . . . whether this thing be set up in his heart, house, or [conduct].

Then Faithful stepped forward again, and said to Talkative, Come, what cheer? How is it now?

TALKATIVE. Thank you, well. I thought we should have had a great deal of talk by this time.

FAITHFUL. Well, if you will, we will fall to it now; and since you left it with me to state the question, let it be this: How doth the saving grace of God discover itself when it is in the heart of man?

TALKATIVE. . . . Well, it is a very good question . . . and take my answer in brief, thus: First, where the grace of God is in the heart, it causeth there a great outcry against sin. Secondly—

FAITHFUL. Nay, hold; let us consider of one at once. I think you should rather say, It shows itself by inclining the soul to abhor its sin.

TALKATIVE. Why, what difference is there between crying out against, and abhorring of sin?

FAITHFUL. Oh! a great deal. A man may cry out against sin [formally], but he cannot abhor it but by virtue of a godly antipathy against it. I have heard many cry out against sin in the pulpit, who yet can abide it well enough in the heart, house and [conduct] . . .

TALKATIVE. You lie at the catch, I perceive.

FAITHFUL. No, not I; I am only for setting things right. But what is the second thing whereby you would prove a discovery of a work of grace in the heart?

TALKATIVE. Great knowledge of gospel mysteries.

FAITHFUL. This sign should have been first: but, first or last, it is also false; for knowledge, great knowledge, may be obtained in the mysteries of the gospel, and yet no work of grace in the soul . . . A work of grace in the soul discovereth itself either to him that hath it, or to standers by.

To him that hath it, thus: It gives him conviction of sin, especially of the defilement of his nature and the sin of unbelief, for the sake of which he is sure to be damned, if he findeth not mercy at God's hand, by faith in Jesus Christ . . . This sight and sense of things worketh in him sorrow and shame for sin; he findeth, moreover, revealed in him the Saviour of the world, and the absolute necessity of closing with Him for life: at the which he findeth hungerings and thirstings after Him . . . Now, according to the strength or weakness of his faith in his Saviour, so is his joy and peace, so is his love to holiness, so are his desires to know Him more, and also to serve Him in this world . . .

To others it is thus discovered:—

> First, By an experimental confession of faith in Christ. Secondly, By a life answerable to that confession: to wit, a life of holiness; heart-holiness, family-holiness, (if he hath a family), and by [conduct-]holiness in the world, which, in the general, teacheth him inwardly to abhor his sin, and himself for that, in secret; to suppress it in his family, and to promote holiness in the world: not by talk only, as a hypocrite or talkative person may do, but by a practical subjection, in faith and love, to the power of the Word [of God] . . . Do you experience this first part of the [work of grace]? and doth your life and [conduct] testify the same? or standeth your religion in word or tongue, and not in deed and truth? Pray, if you incline to answer me in this, say no more than you know the God above will say Amen to; and, also, nothing but what your conscience can justify you in: 'for not he that commendeth himself is approved, but whom the Lord commendeth.' Besides, to say I am thus and thus, when my [conduct], and all my neighbors, tell me I lie, is great wickedness.

TALKATIVE. Then Talkative at first began to blush; but, recovering himself, he thus replied: You come now to experience, to conscience, and God . . . This kind of discourse I did not expect; nor am I disposed to give an answer to such questions . . . But, I pray, will you tell me why you ask me such questions?

FAITHFUL. Because I saw you forward to talk, and because I knew not that you had aught else but notion. Besides, to tell you the truth, I have heard of you that you are a man whose religion lies in talk, and that your [conduct] gives this your mouth profession the lie. They say you are a spot among Christians; and that religion fareth the worse for your ungodly [conduct]; that some have already stumbled at your wicked ways, and that more are in danger of being destroyed thereby; your religion, and an alehouse, and covetousness, and uncleanness, and swearing, and lying, and vain company-keeping, etc., will stand together. The proverb is true of you which is said of a whore, to wit, that 'she is a shame to all women.' So you are a shame to all [Christians].

TALKATIVE. Since you are so ready to take up reports, and to judge so rashly as you do, I cannot but conclude you are some peevish or melancholic man, not fit to be discoursed with; and so adieu.

CHRISTIAN. Then came up Christian and said to his brother, I told you how it would happen; your words and his lusts could not agree. He had rather leave your company than reform his life. But he is gone, as I said; let him go, the loss is no man's but his own. He has saved us the trouble of going from him; for he continuing (as I suppose he will do) as he is, he would have been but a blot in our company: besides, the apostle says, 'From such withdraw thyself.'

FAITHFUL. But I am glad we had this little discourse with him; it may happen that he will think of it again: however, I have dealt plainly with him, and so am clear of his blood if he perisheth.

CHRISTIAN. You did well to talk so plainly to him as you did. There is but little of this faithful dealing with men nowadays, and that makes religion to stink in the nostrils of so many as it doth: for they are these talkative fools whose religion is only in word, and are debauched and vain in their [conduct], that (being so much admitted into the fellowship of the godly) do puzzle the world, blemish Christianity, and grieve the sincere. I wish that all men would deal with such as you have done; then should they either be made more conformable to religion, or the company of [believers] would be too hot for them. Then did Faithful say—

> How Talkative at first lifts up his plumes!
> How bravely doth he speak! How he presumes
> To drive down all before him! But so soon
> As Faithful talks of heart-work, like the moon
> That's past the full, into the wane he goes;
> And so will all but he that heart-work knows.

How have the myths of our nation's founding taken such a strong hold on our imagination? And why do they persist so powerfully even to this day?

First, our ancestors demonstrated to a remarkable degree a knack for what we call spinning. "Americans mastered the use of propaganda from the beginning: their ability to present their case in terms of impeccable righteousness . . . was second to none . . . Exaggeration and misinformation were vital in order to boost support among the American people, frighten domestic enemies, and demoralize a British war effort that had only the half-hearted approval of public opinion at home"[122].

"They make ready their tongue like a bow, to shoot lies; it is not by truth that they triumph in the land. They go from one sin to another; they do not acknowledge me,' declares the Lord" (Jeremiah 9:3). "For the time will come when men will not put up with sound doctrine. Instead, to suit their own desires, they will gather around them a great number of teachers to say what their itching ears want to hear. They will turn their ears away from the truth and turn aside to myths" (II Timothy 4:3-4). But they did acknowledge a god of their own making, a sort of divine Step-n-Fetchit, the detached god of Deism. Ironically, this god didn't care to fetch anything, because he simply didn't give two hoots about human beings at all. Asking the Deist god, the Supreme Watchmaker who wound up the world and then skedaddled, to pay attention to it, to drill all the way down into the boring details of the founding of some rinky-dink lil' country or other, *might* elicit a guffaw from him but for the fact that he wouldn't have listened to the request in the first place. But the true God *does* care about our affairs "and even the very hairs of your head are all numbered" (Matthew 10:30).

Secondly, most of today's Christian leaders judge the Founding Fathers according to their words, not by what they did. However "even a child is known by his actions, by whether his conduct is pure and right" (Proverbs 20:11). We would do well to heed the words of Jesus: "Stop judging by mere appearances, and make a right judgment" (John 7:24).

"They cling to deceit; they refuse to return. I have listened attentively, but they do not say what is right. No one repents of his wickedness, saying, 'What have I done?' Each pursues his own course like a horse charging into battle. Even the stork in the sky knows her appointed seasons, and the dove, the swift and the thrush observe the time of their migration. But my people do not know the requirements of the Lord" (Jeremiah 8:5-7).

"Can a corrupt throne be allied with [God]—one that brings on misery by its decrees?" (Psalm 94:20). "They have built the high places of Topheth in the Valley of Ben Hinnom to burn their sons and daughters in the fire—something I did not command nor did it enter my mind" (Jeremiah 7:31). Renaming our Topheths reproductive health clinics and tweaking the method of child sacrifice helps us forget the misery we bring to our loved ones and even to ourselves, but the first step in repentance is not to forget. "The Lord is close to the broken-hearted and saves those who are crushed in spirit" (Psalm 34:18). "The sacrifices of God are a broken spirit; a broken and contrite heart, O God, you will not despise" (Psalm 51:17). "Rend your heart and not your garments. Return to the Lord your God, for he is gracious and compassionate, slow to anger and abounding in love, and he relents from sending calamity" (Joel 2:13). "Godly sorrow brings repentance that leads to salvation and leaves no regret" (II Corinthians 7:10). Then the words of the prophet will come true for you: "The Lord your God is with you, he is mighty to save. He will take great delight in you, he will quiet you with his love, he will rejoice over you with singing" (Zephaniah 3:17). Genuine spiritual revival starts not by force of law from the top down, but at the grass-roots level with conviction of sin in the hearts of individuals.

"This is what the Lord says: 'Let not the wise man boast of his wisdom or the strong man boast of his strength or the rich man boast of his riches [might I add 'let not the patriot boast of his country'?], but let him who boasts boast about this: that he understands and knows me, that I am the Lord, who exercises kindness, justice and righteousness on earth, for in these I delight,' declares the Lord" (Jeremiah 9:23-24).

Two citizens of India, worshipers of Allah, stood chatting in a village marketplace, bemoaning the state of their beloved country.

"Allah be praised," intoned Abdullah.

"Would that it were so!" exclaimed Saeed forlornly. "The name of Allah, the merciful and compassionate, is so little regarded these days."

"It was different in the old days," blurted out Abdullah after a moment's somber reflection. Absentmindedly he tossed a stone that ricocheted off a wagon wheel and knocked over a wind-up musical toy in a vendor's kiosk. Attracted by the tune it began to play, Nozzle the baby elephant came trotting up to investigate. With her agile trunk she sniffed and blew on it gently in turn and wrinkled her mouth in a grin both mischievous and goofy.

"All these millions of Hindu gods," sighed Saeed, as Nozzle waved the toy in front of him. He took it from her outstretched appendage and examined it. "Here's one right here. Ganesh," as he held it up for his friend to see. "But who worships Allah these days?" He sighed deeply and returned it to the kiosk without interrupting the merchant's peaceful nap, setting it carefully in its place. "May his name be praised."

"Ganesh?" asked Abdullah worriedly.

"No, no, I meant Allah" explained the other. They smiled knowingly at each other. Nozzle, still standing in front of the pair, grinned too and snatched a pen out of Saeed's shirt pocket and offered it to Abdullah who handed it back to Saeed. She reached confidently into Abdullah's shirt pocket and gave his bubble gum to Saeed who handed it back to its owner. The pencil behind an ear was next and in fairly quick succession a pocket watch, a Swiss army knife, a key chain, deodorant, toothbrush, lip balm and—of course—their Korans. (But when Saeed got home that night he found his key incapable of unlocking the door and Abdullah's wife eyed a strange toothbrush suspiciously the next morning in the bathroom. But who can keep up with that nozzle?)

The handing back of items expended a good deal of energy—there'd been multiple takings by Nozzle of the same things—so the men panted and wiped their brows with the backs of their wrists. (Two handkerchiefs draped across the unsuspecting nearby napper's chest). The playful pachyderm still sported that goofily mischievous grin.

"What our beautiful country needs, Abdullah," continued Saeed in deep earnest when he'd caught his breath, "is the return of the Mughals." A couple of passing Hindus overheard this heartfelt remark and stopped to listen in astonishment. "*That* was a time when India followed the one true God."

"May his name be forever praised," agreed Abdullah.

"We *must* return to our nation's historical roots!" The Hindus, even more surprised, dropped their jaws. As the devout Muslims trudged off into the sunset, the Hindus spoke in low tones of amazement.

"What's this about 'historical roots'?!?!" exclaimed Raj.

"We were here first!!" cried Ramesh. "Shoo, Nozzle! Give that back! . . . Whose hankie is this?"

As the Muslims were to the Hindus, so are American Christians to the First Americans. And besides, if peoples should return to their roots, then Africa should return to animism, the British to Druidism, the Chinese to Taoism, southern Europeans to the Roman or Greek gods and the United States either to Deism or the Great Spirit. What a shock to Christians it would be if Satan gleefully supported a return to our roots!

CHAPTER 4

POLITICAL QUIETISM:

ENEMY OF THE WHORE OF BABYLON

"Then the angel carried me away in the Spirit into a desert. There I saw a woman sitting on a scarlet beast that was covered with blasphemous names and had seven heads and ten horns. The woman was dressed in purple and scarlet, and was glittering with gold, precious stones and pearls. She held a golden cup in her hand, filled with abominable things and the filth of her adulteries. This title was written on her forehead:

> MYSTERY
> BABYLON THE GREAT
> THE MOTHER OF PROSTITUTES
> AND OF THE ABOMINATIONS OF THE EARTH.

I saw that the woman was drunk with the blood of the saints, the blood of those who bore testimony to Jesus" (Revelation 17:3-6).

Samuel Taylor Coleridge makes this penetrating comment about this passage: "I am convinced that the Babylon of the Apocalypse does . . . apply . . . to the union of Religion with Power and Wealth, wherever it is found"[123].

Archbishop Leighton of the Church of England described the nexus between religion and politics in a manner not likely to win the Christian Coalition's approval:

> "The too ardent love or self-willed desire of power, or wealth,
> or credit in the world, is (an Apostle has assured us) Idolatry.

Now among the words or synonyms for idols, in the Hebrew language, there is one that in its primary sense signifies 'troubles' (*tegirim*), other two that signify 'terrors' (*miphletzeth* and *emim*). And so it is certainly. All our idols prove so to us. They fill us with nothing but anguish and troubles, with cares and fears, that are good for nothing but to be fit punishments of the folly, out of which they arise"[124].

Now, if my reader has made her peace with God and entered into a personal relationship with Him as her Lord and Savior, please allow Leighton's thoughts on coping with fear to comfort you in these troubled times:

"Our condition is universally exposed to fears and troubles, and no man is so stupid but he studies and projects for some fence against them, some bulwark to break the incursion of evils, and so to bring his mind to some ease, ridding it of the fear of them. Thus men seek safety in the greatness, or multitude, or supposed faithfulness of friends; they seek by any means to be strongly underset this way; to have many, and powerful, and trustworthy friends. But wiser men, perceiving the unsafety and vanity of these and all external things, have cast about for some higher course. They see a necessity of withdrawing a man from externals, which do nothing but mock and deceive those most who trust most to them; but they cannot tell where to direct him. The best of them bring him *into himself*, and think to quiet him so; but the truth is, he finds as little to support him there; there is nothing truly strong enough within him, to hold out against the many sorrows and fears which still from without do assault him. So then, though it is well done, to call off a man from outward things, as moving sands, that he build not on them, yet, this is not enough; for his own spirit is as unsettled a piece as is in all the world, and must have some higher strength than its own, to fortify and fix it. This is the way that is here taught, *Fear not their fear, but sanctify the Lord your God in your hearts*; and if you can attain this latter, the former will follow of itself"[125].

What was the stance of early American Christians on involvement in politics? Cotton Mather (1663-1728), a devout Puritan and eminent theologian and historian, wrote a book called *Bonifacius* [On Doing Good] in which he treats of proper Christian behavior in the community and encouraged the formation of social clubs for young men.

> "Let the whole [club] be exceedingly careful, that their discourse while they are together, after the other services of religion are over, have nothing in it, that shall have any taint of backbiting or vanity, *or the least relation to the affairs of government*, or to things which do not concern them, and do not serve the interests of holiness in their own conversation. But let their discourse be wholly on the matters of religion; and those also, not the disputable and controversial matters, but the points of practical piety . . . Once in two months, let the whole time of the meeting, be devoted unto supplications for the . . . salvation of the rising generation in the land; and particularly, for the success of the Gospel in that congregation [to which] the [club] does belong"[126].

Although a democratic form of government calls for more citizen participation than would've been possible in Mather's day, there's a distinction between casting a vote and seeking to dominate the country, an ironic urge given the status of Christians (not nominal but true believers) as a deviant subculture from the perspective of the majority.

Would Coleridge's tender conscience in matters of faith, politics and war so movingly displayed in his poem "Religious Musings[127]," written on Christmas Eve 1794, elicit the disapproval of the world's Talkatives? Here are some excerpts from an author whom *I* don't consider a fool or blockhead but rather a deeply spiritual man:

> *This is the time, when most divine to hear,*
> *The voice of adoration rouses me,*
> *As with a Cherub's trump: and high upborne,*
> *Yea, mingling with the choir, I seem to view*
> *The vision of the heavenly multitude,*
> *Who hymned the song of peace o'er Bethlehem's fields!*
> *Yet thou more bright than all the angel blaze,*

That harbingered thy birth, Thou, Man of Woes!
Despised Galilean! For the great
Invisible (by symbols only seen)
With a peculiar and surpassing light
Shines from the visage of the oppressed good man,
When heedless of himself the scourged Saint
Mourns for the oppressor. Fair the vernal mead,
Fair the high grove, the sea, the sun, the stars;
True impress each of their creating Sire!
Yet nor high grove, nor many-coloured mead,
Nor the green Ocean with his thousand isles,
Nor the starred azure, nor the sovran sun,
E'er with such majesty of portraiture
Imaged the supreme beauty uncreate,
As thou, meek Saviour! at the fearful hour
When thy insulted anguish winged the prayer
Harped by Archangels, when they sing of mercy!
Which when the Almighty heard from forth his throne
Diviner light filled Heaven with ecstasy!
Heaven's hymnings paused: and Hell her yawning mouth
Closed a brief moment.

Lovely was the death
Of Him whose life was Love! Holy with power
He on the thought-benighted Sceptic beamed
Manifest Godhead, melting into day
What floating mists of dark idolatry
Broke and misshaped the omnipresent Sire . . .

And blest are they,
Who in this fleshly World, the elect of Heaven,
Their strong eye darting through the deeds of men,
Adore with steadfast unpresuming gaze
Him Nature's essence, mind, and energy!
And gazing, trembling, patiently ascend
Treading beneath their feet all visible things
As steps, that upward to their Father's throne
Lead gradual—else nor glorified nor loved.
They nor contempt embosom nor revenge

    . . . *Who the Creator love, created might*[128]
Dread not: within their tents no terrors walk.
For they are holy things before the Lord
Aye unprofaned, though Earth should league with Hell;
God's altar grasping with an eager hand
Fear, the wild-visaged, pale, eye-starting wretch,
Sure-refug'd hears his hot pursuing fiends
Yell at vain distance. Soon refreshed from Heaven
He calms the throb and tempest of his heart.
His countenance settles; a soft solemn bliss
Swims in his eye—his swimming eye upraised:
And Faith's whole armour glitters on his limbs!
And thus transfigured with a dreadless awe,
A solemn hush of soul, meek he beholds
All things of terrible seeming: yea, unmoved
Views e'en the immitigable ministers
That shower down vengeance on these latter days.

    . . . *Thus from the Elect, regenerate through faith,*
Pass the dark Passions and what thirsty Cares[129]
Drink up the Spirit . . .

There is one Mind, one omnipresent Mind,
Omnific. His most holy name is Love.
Truth of subliming import! with the which
Who feeds and saturates his constant soul,
He from his small particular orbit flies
With blest outstarting! From himself he flies,
Stands in the sun, and with no partial gaze
Views all creation; and he loves it all,
And blesses it, and calls it very good!
This is indeed to dwell with the most High!
Cherubs and rapture-trembling Seraphim
Can press no nearer to the Almighty's Throne.
But that we roam unconscious, or with hearts
Unfeeling of our universal Sire,

And that in his vast family no Cain
Injures uninjured (in her best-aimed blow
Victorious murder a blind suicide)
Haply for this some younger Angel now
Looks down on human nature: and, behold!
A sea of blood bestrewed with wrecks, where mad
Embattling interests on each other rush
With unhelmed rage!

        'Tis the sublime of man,
Our noontide majesty, to know ourselves
Parts and proportions of one wondrous whole!
This fraternises man, this constitutes
Our charities and bearings. But 'tis God
Diffused through all, that doth make all one whole;
This the worst superstition, him except
Aught to desire,[130] Supreme Reality!
The plenitude and permanence of bliss!
O Fiends of Superstition! not that oft
The erring priest hath stained with brother's blood
Your grisly idols, not for this may wrath
Thunder against you from the Holy One!
But o'er some plain that steameth to the sun,
Peopled with death; or where more hideous Trade
Loud-laughing packs his bales of human anguish;
I will raise up a mourning, O ye Fiends!
And curse your spells, that film the eye of Faith,
Hiding the present God; whose presence lost,
The moral world's cohesion, we become
An anarchy of Spirits! Toy-bewitched,
Made blind by lusts,[131] disherited of soul,
No common center Man, no common sire
Knoweth! A sordid solitary thing,
Mid countless brethren with a lonely heart
Through courts and cities the smooth savage roams
Feeling himself, his own low self the whole;
When he by sacred sympathy might make

The whole one self! Self, that no alien knows!
Self, far diffused as Fancy's wing can travel!
Self, spreading still! Oblivious of its own,
Yet all of all possessing! This is Faith!
This the Messiah's destined victory!

But first offences needs must come! Even now
(Black Hell laughs horrible—to hear the scoff!)
Thee to defend, meek Galilean! Thee
And thy mild laws of Love unutterable,
Mistrust and enmity have burst the bands
Of social peace: and listening treachery lurks
With pious fraud to snare a brother's life;
And childless widows o'er the groaning land
Wail numberless; and orphans weep for bread
Thee to defend, dear Saviour of mankind!
Thee, Lamb of God! Thee, blameless Prince of peace!
From all sides rush the thirsty brood of War

. . . Soul-hardened barterers of human blood!
Death's prime slave-merchants! Scorpion-whips of Fate!
Nor least in savagery of holy zeal
. . . Thee to defend the Moloch priest prefers
The prayer of hate, and bellows to the herd,
That Deity, accomplice Deity
In the fierce jealousy of wakened wrath
Will go forth with our armies and our fleets
To scatter the red ruin on their foes!
O blasphemy![132] to mingle fiendish deeds
With blessedness! . . .

O ye numberless,
Whom foul oppression's ruffian gluttony
Drives from life's plenteous feast! O thou poor wretch
Who nursed in darkness and made wild by want,
Roamest for prey, yea thy unnatural hand
Dost lift to deeds of blood! O pale-eyed form,
The victim of seduction, doomed to know
Polluted nights and days of blasphemy;

Who in loathed orgies with lewd wassailers
Must gaily laugh, while thy remembered home
Gnaws like a viper at thy secret heart!
O aged women! ye who weekly catch
The morsel tossed by law-forced charity,
And die so slowly, that none call it murder!
O loathly suppliants! ye, that unreceived
Totter heart-broken from the closing gates
Of the full Lazar-house:[133]or, gazing, stand
Sick with despair! O ye to glory's field
Forced or ensnared, who, as ye gasp in death,
Bleed with new wounds beneath the vulture's beak!
O thou poor widow, who in dreams dost view
Thy husband's mangled corse,[134] and from short doze
Start'st with a shriek; or in thy half-thatched cot
Waked by the wintry night-storm, wet and cold,
Cow'rst o'er thy screaming baby! Rest awhile
Children of wretchedness! More groans must rise,
More blood must stream, or ere your wrongs be full.
Yet is the day of retribution nigh:
The Lamb of God hath opened the fifth seal:[135]
And upward rush on swiftest wing of fire
The innumerable multitude of Wrongs
By man on man inflicted! Rest awhile,
Children of wretchedness! The hour is nigh;
And lo! the great, the rich, the mighty Men,
The Kings and the chief Captains of the World,
With all that fixed on high like stars of Heaven
Shot baleful influence, shall be cast to earth,
Vile and down-trodden, as the untimely fruit
Shook from the fig-tree by a sudden storm.
Even now the storm begins: each gentle name,
Faith and meek Piety, with fearful joy
Tremble far-off—for lo! the giant Frenzy
Uprooting empires with his whirlwind arm
Mocketh high Heaven; burst hideous from the cell
Where the old Hag, unconquerable, huge,
Creation's eyeless drudge, black ruin, sits
Nursing the impatient earthquake.

O return!
Pure Faith! meek Piety! The abhorred Form
Whose scarlet robe was stiff with earthly pomp,
Who drank iniquity in cups of gold,
Whose names were many and all blasphemous,
Hath met the horrible judgment! Whence that cry?
The mighty army of foul Spirits shrieked
Disherited of earth! For she hath fallen
On whose black front was written Mystery;
She that reeled heavily, whose wine was blood;
She that worked whoredom with the Demon Power,
And from the dark embrace all evil things
Brought forth and nurtured . . .

Return pure Faith! return meek Piety! . . .
Such delights as float to earth, permitted visitants!
When in some hour of solemn jubilee
The massy gates of Paradise are thrown
Wide open, and forth come in fragments wild
Sweet echoes of unearthly melodies,
And odours snatched from beds of amaranth,
And they, that from the crystal river of life
Spring up on freshened wing, ambrosial gales!
The favoured good man in his lonely walk
Perceives them, and his silent spirit drinks
Strange bliss which he shall recognise in heaven.
And such delights, such strange beatitudes
Seize on my young anticipating heart
When that blest future rushes on my view!
For in his own and in his Father's might
The Saviour comes! While as the Thousand Years
Lead up their mystic dance, the Desert shouts!
Old Ocean claps his hands! The mighty Dead
Rise to new life, whoe'er from earliest time
With conscious zeal had urged Love's wondrous plan,
Coadjutors of God.

> *. . . Who of woman born*
> *May image in the workings of his thought,*
> *How the black-visaged, red-eyed Fiend outstretched*
> *Beneath the unsteady feet of Nature groans,*
> *In feverous slumbers—destined then to wake,*
> *When fiery whirlwinds thunder his dread name*
> *And Angels shout, Destruction! . . .*
>
> *Believe thou, O my soul,*
> *Life is a vision shadowy of Truth;*
> *And vice, and anguish, and the wormy grave,*
> *Shapes of a dream! The veiling clouds retire,*
> *And lo! the Throne of the redeeming God*
> *Forth flashing unimaginable day*
> *Wraps in one blaze earth, heaven, and deepest hell.*
>
> *Contemplant Spirits! ye that hover o'er*
> *With untired gaze the immeasurable fount*
> *Ebullient with creative Deity! . . .*
> *I haply journeying my immortal course*
> *Shall sometime join your mystic choir. Till then*
> *I discipline my young and novice thought*
> *In ministeries of heart-stirring song,*
> *And aye on Meditation's heaven-ward wing*
> *Soaring aloft I breathe the empyreal air*
> *Of Love, omnific, omnipresent Love,*
> *Whose day-spring rises glorious in my soul*
> *As the great Sun, when he his influence*
> *Sheds on the frost-bound waters—The glad stream*
> *Flows to the ray and warbles as it flows."*

Tradition has it that Mohammed, according to Ghazali, wanted the *ulama* (Muslim scholars) to keep their distance from political figures.

> "'In Hell,' said Mohammed, 'there is a valley uniquely reserved
> for *ulama* who visit kings.' The virtuous [scholar] should not

visit unjust princes or officials. He could visit a just ruler, but without subservience, and should reproach him if he saw him doing anything reprehensible; if he was afraid he could keep silent, but it would be better not to visit him at all. If he received a visit from a prince, he should return his salutation and exhort him to virtue. It would be better, however, to avoid him altogether"[136].

CHAPTER 5

IS GOD ANTI-SEMITIC?

"Do not oppress an alien; you yourselves know how it feels to be aliens, because you were aliens in Egypt" (Exodus 23:9).

"When Moses approached the camp and saw the [golden] calf..., his anger burned.... 'Do not be angry, my lord,' Aaron answered. 'You know how prone these people are to evil. They said to me, 'Make us gods who will go before us' ... Moses saw that the people were running wild and that Aaron had let them get out of control and so become a laughingstock to their enemies. So he stood at the entrance to the camp and said, 'Whoever is for the Lord, come to me.' And all the Levites rallied to him. Then he said to them, 'This is what the Lord, the God of Israel, says: 'Each man strap a sword to his side. Go back and forth through the camp from one end to the other, each killing his brother and friend and neighbor.' The Levites did as Moses commanded, and that day about three thousand of the people died. Then Moses said, 'You have been set apart to the Lord today, for you were against your own sons and brothers, and he has blessed you this day'" (Exodus 32:19, 22, 23, 25-29).

"Then the Lord said to Moses, 'Leave this place, you and the people you brought up out of Egypt, and go up to the land I promised on oath to Abraham, Isaac and Jacob, saying, 'I will give it to your descendants' ... But I will not go with you, because you are a stiff-necked people and I might destroy you on the way'" (Exodus 33:1, 3).

"Now the people complained about their hardships in the hearing of the Lord, and when he heard them his anger was aroused. Then fire from the Lord burned among them and consumed some of the outskirts of the camp" (Numbers 11:1).

"The rabble with them began to crave other food, and again the Israelites started wailing and said, 'If only we had meat to eat! We remember the fish we ate in Egypt at no cost—also the cucumbers, melons, leeks, onions and garlic. But now we have lost our appetite; we never see anything but this manna!' The Lord became exceedingly angry, and Moses was troubled. 'Tell the people: 'Consecrate yourselves in preparation for tomorrow, when you will eat meat. You will not eat it for just one day, or two days, or five, ten or twenty days, but for a whole month—until it comes out of your nostrils and you loathe it—because you have rejected the Lord . . . and have wailed before him, saying, 'Why did we ever leave Egypt?'" (Numbers 11:4-5, 10, 18, 19-20).

"The Lord said to Moses, 'How long will these people treat me with contempt? How long will they refuse to believe in me, in spite of all the miraculous signs I have performed among them? How long will this wicked community grumble against me? So tell them, 'As surely as I live . . . I will do to you the very things I heard you say: In this desert your bodies will fall—every one of you twenty years old or more who . . . has grumbled against me. Not one of you will enter the land I swore with uplifted hand to make your home, except Caleb son of Jephunneh and Joshua son of Nun. Your children will be shepherds here for forty years, suffering for your unfaithfulness, until the last of your bodies lies in the desert'" (Numbers 14:11, 27, 28, 29, 30, 33).

"Korah . . . and certain Reubenites—Dathan and Abiram . . . became insolent and rose up against Moses. With them were 250 Israelite men, well-known community leaders . . . Then the Lord said to Moses, 'Say to the assembly, 'Move away from the tents of Korah, Dathan and Abiram.' [T]he ground under them split apart and the earth opened its mouth and swallowed them, with their households and all Korah's men . . . . And fire came out from the Lord and consumed the 250 men. The next day the whole Israelite community grumbled against Moses and Aaron. 'You have killed the Lord's people,' they said. [T]he Lord said to Moses, 'Get away from this assembly so I can put an end to them at once.' [Aaron] stood between the living and the dead, and the plague stopped. But 14,700 people died from the plague, in addition to those who had died because of Korah" (Numbers 16:1, 2, 23-24, 31, 32, 35, 41, 44, 45, 48-49).

"They traveled from Mount Hor along the route to the Red Sea, to go around Edom. But the people grew impatient on the way; they spoke against God and against Moses, and said, 'Why have you brought us up out of Egypt to die in the desert? There is no bread! There is no water! And we detest this miserable food!' Then the Lord sent venomous snakes among them; they bit the people and many Israelites died" (Numbers 21:4-6).

"While Israel was staying in Shittim, the men began to indulge in sexual immorality with Moabite women, who invited them to the sacrifices to their gods. The people ate and bowed down before these gods. And the Lord's anger burned against them. [T]hose who died in the plague numbered 24,000" (Numbers 25:1-2, 3, 9).

"After the Lord your God has driven [the original tribes of the promised land] out before you, do not say to yourself, 'The Lord has brought me here to take possession of this land because of my righteousness.' No, it is on account of the wickedness of these nations that the Lord is going to drive them out before you. Understand, then, that it is not because of your righteousness that the Lord your God is giving you this good land to possess, for you are a stiff-necked people" (Deuteronomy 9:4,6). "[H]e gave them the lands of the nations . . . that they might keep his precepts and observe his laws" (Psalm 105:44-45).

"The Lord sent Babylonian, Aramean, Moabite and Ammonite raiders against [Jehoiakim, king of Judah]. He sent them to destroy Judah, in accordance with the word of the Lord proclaimed by his servants the prophets. Surely these things happened to Judah according to the Lord's command, in order to remove them from his presence because of the sins of [King] Manasseh and all he had done, including the shedding of innocent blood. For he had filled Jerusalem with innocent blood, and the Lord was not willing to forgive" (II Kings 24:2-4).

"My people are fools; they do not know me. They are senseless children; they have no understanding. They are skilled in doing evil; they know not how to do good" (Jeremiah 4:22).

"'The days are coming,' declared the Lord, 'when I will punish all who are circumcised only in the flesh—Egypt, Judah, Edom, Ammon, Moab and all who live in the desert in distant places. For all these nations are really uncircumcised, and even the whole house of Israel is uncircumcised in heart'" (Jeremiah 9:25-26).

"And the Lord said to Moses: 'You are going to rest with your fathers, and these people will soon prostitute themselves to the foreign gods of the land they are entering. They will forsake me and break the covenant I made with them. On that day I will become angry with them and forsake them; I will hide my face from them, and they will be destroyed. Many disasters and difficulties will come upon them, and on that day they will ask, 'Have not these disasters come upon us because our God is not with us?'" (Deuteronomy 31:16-17).

"Hear, O heavens! Listen, O earth! For the Lord has spoken: 'I reared children and brought them up, but they have rebelled against me. The ox knows his master, the donkey his owner's manger, but Israel does not know, my people do not understand.' Ah, sinful nation, a people loaded with guilt, a brood of evildoers, children given to corruption. Why should you be beaten anymore? Why do you persist in rebellion? Your whole head is injured, your whole heart afflicted. Your country is desolate, your cities burned with fire; your fields are being stripped by foreigners right before you, laid waste as when overthrown by strangers. Unless the Lord Almighty had left us some survivors, we would have become like Sodom . . . and Gomorrah" (Isaiah 1: 2-3, 4, 5, 7, 9).

"'What more could have been done for my vineyard than I have done for it? When I looked for good grapes, why did it yield only bad? Now I will tell you what I am going to do to my vineyard: I will take away its hedge, and it will be destroyed; I will break down its wall, and it will be trampled. The vineyard of the Lord Almighty is the house of Israel and the men of Judah are the garden of his delight. And he looked for justice, but saw bloodshed; for righteousness, but heard cries of distress" (Isaiah 5:4-5, 7).

"'Are not you Israelites the same to me as the Cushites?' declares the Lord. 'Did I not bring Israel up from Egypt, the Philistines from Caphtor and the Arameans from Kir?'" (Amos 9:7).

"Hear the word of the Lord, you Israelites, because the Lord has a charge to bring against you . . . : 'There is no faithfulness, no love, no acknowledgement of God in the land. There is only cursing, lying and murder, stealing and adultery; they break all bounds, and bloodshed follows bloodshed. [M]y people are destroyed from lack of knowledge. [B]ecause you have ignored the law of your God, I also will ignore your children. Do not go to Gilgal; do not go up to Beth Aven. And do not swear, 'As surely as the Lord lives!' The Israelites are stubborn, like a stubborn heifer. How then can the Lord pasture them like lambs in a meadow? A whirlwind will sweep them away, and their sacrifices will bring them shame" (Hosea 4:1-2, 6, 15, 16, 19).

"Israel's arrogance testifies against him, but despite all this he does not return to the Lord his God or search for him. I long to redeem them but they speak lies against me. They do not cry out to me from their hearts but wail upon their beds. Their leaders will fall by the sword because of their insolent words" (Hosea 7:10, 13, 14, 16).

"[Y]ou have eaten the fruit of deception. Because you have depended on your own strength and on your many warriors, the roar of battle will rise against your people, so that all your fortresses will be devastated" (Hosea 10:13, 14).

"They willfully put God to the test by demanding the food they craved. They spoke against God, saying, 'Can God spread a table in the desert? When he struck the rock, water gushed out, and streams flowed abundantly. But can he also give us food? Can he supply meat for his people?' When the Lord heard them, he was very angry . . . for they did not . . . trust in his deliverance. In spite of all this, they kept on sinning; in spite of his wonders, they did not believe. So he ended their days in futility and their years in terror. Whenever God slew them, they would seek him. But then they would flatter him with their mouths, lying to him with their tongues; their hearts were not loyal to him. Yet he was merciful; he atoned for their iniquities and did not destroy them. Time after time he restrained his anger and did not stir up his full wrath. He remembered that they were but flesh" (Psalm 78:18-20, 21, 22, 32-33, 34, 36, 37, 38, 39).

"'If my people would but listen to me, if Israel would follow my ways, how quickly would I subdue their enemies and turn my hand against their foes!'" (Psalm 81:13-14).

"'If... you still do not listen to me but continue to be hostile toward me, ... I will ... pile your dead bodies on the lifeless forms of your idols, and I will abhor you. I will turn your cities into ruins and lay waste your sanctuaries. I will lay waste the land. I will scatter you among the nations and will draw out my sword and pursue you. Then the land will enjoy its sabbath years all the time that it lies desolate and you are in the country of your enemies. [It] will have the rest it did not have during the sabbaths you lived in it" (Leviticus 26:27, 30, 31, 32, 33, 34, 35).

"In that day the remnant of Israel ... will truly rely on the Lord, the Holy One of Israel. Though your people, O Israel, be like the sand by the sea, only a remnant will return" (Isaiah 10:20, 22).

"The Lord says: 'These people come near to me with their mouth and honor me with their lips, but their hearts are far from me. Their worship of me is made up only of rules taught by men'" (Isaiah 29:13).

"The sinners in Zion are terrified; trembling grips the godless: 'Who of us can dwell with the consuming fire?' He who walks righteously and speaks what is right, who rejects gain from extortion and keeps his hand from accepting bribes, who stops his ears against plots of murder and shuts his eyes against contemplating evil—this is the man who will dwell on the heights, whose refuge will be the mountain fortress. His bread will be supplied, and water will not fail him" (Isaiah 33:14, 15-16).

"'Is not this the kind of fasting I have chosen: to loose the chains of injustice and untie the cords of the yoke, to set the oppressed free and break every yoke?'" (Isaiah 58:6).

"Yet they rebelled and grieved his Holy Spirit. So he turned and became their enemy and he himself fought against them" (Isaiah 63:10).

"All of us have become like one who is unclean, and all our righteous acts are like filthy rags" (Isaiah 64:6).

"When I fed them, they were satisfied; when they were satisfied, they became proud; then they forgot me" (Hosea 13:6).

"This is what the Lord says: 'For three sins of Israel, even for four, I will not turn back my wrath. They sell the righteous for silver, and the needy for a pair of sandals. They trample on the heads of the poor as upon the dust of the ground and deny justice to the oppressed. Father and son use the same girl and so profane my holy name. They lie down beside every altar on garments taken in pledge. In the house of their god they drink wine taken as fines'" (Amos 2:6-8).

"'Burn leavened bread as a thank offering and brag about your freewill offerings—boast about them, you Israelites, for this is what you love to do,' declares the Sovereign Lord" (Amos 4:5).

"I hate, I despise your religious feasts; I cannot stand your assemblies. Even though you bring me burnt offerings and grain offerings, I will not accept them. Though you bring choice fellowship offerings, I will have no regard for them. Away with the noise of your songs! I will not listen to the music of your harps. But let justice roll on like a river, righteousness like a never-failing stream!" (Amos 5:21-24).

"At that time I will search Jerusalem with lamps and punish those who are complacent, who think, 'The Lord will do nothing, either good or bad'" (Zephaniah 1:12).

"Seek the Lord, all you humble of the land, you who do what he commands. Seek righteousness, seek humility; perhaps you will be sheltered on the day of the Lord's anger" (Zephaniah 2:3).

"But they refused to pay attention; stubbornly they turned their backs and stopped up their ears. They made their hearts as hard as flint" (Zechariah 7:11,12).

"Go now to the place in Shiloh where I first made a dwelling for my Name, and see what I did to it because of the wickedness of my people Israel. Therefore, what I did to Shiloh I will now do to the house that bears my Name, the temple you trust in" (Jeremiah 7:12,14).

"'And now this admonition is for you, O priests. If you do not listen, and if you do not set your heart to honor my name,' says the Lord Almighty, 'I will send a curse upon you, and I will curse your blessings. Yes, I have already cursed them, because you have not set your heart to honor me. Because of you I will rebuke your descendants; I will spread on your faces the offal from your festival sacrifices, and you will be carried off with it. And you will know that I have sent you this admonition so that my covenant with Levi may continue. My covenant was with him, a covenant of life and peace, and I gave them to him; this called for reverence and he revered me and stood in awe of my name. True instruction was in his mouth and nothing false was found on his lips. He walked with me in peace and uprightness, and turned many from sin. For the lips of a priest ought to preserve knowledge, and from his mouth men should seek instruction—because he is the messenger of the Lord Almighty. But you have turned from the way and by your teaching have caused many to stumble; you have violated the covenant with Levi. So I have caused you to be despised and humiliated before all the people, because you have not followed my ways but have shown partiality in matters of the law'" (Malachi 2:1-9).

"A man is not a Jew if he is only one outwardly, nor is circumcision merely outward and physical. No, a man is a Jew if he is one inwardly; and circumcision is circumcision of the heart, by the Spirit, not by the written code. Such a man's praise is not from men, but from God" (Romans 2:28-29).

"For not all who are descended from Israel are Israel. Nor because they are his descendants are they all Abrahams's children. On the contrary, 'It is through Isaac that your offspring will be reckoned.' In other words, it is not the natural children who are God's children, but it is the children of the promise who are regarded as Abraham's offspring. For this was how the promise was stated: 'At the appointed time I will return, and Sarah will have a son'" (Romans 9:6-9).

CHAPTER 6

WHO ARE GOD'S CHILDREN?

The spirit of Zionism is presumption.

Anti-Zionism, *pace* Chaim Weizmann, a leader of the movement, is not anti-Semitism. In his fascinating book, *One Palestine, Complete: Jews and Arabs under the British Mandate[137]*, Tom Segev, a columnist for *Ha'aretz*, notes that "most Jews did not support Zionism," an organization so inconsequential in 1917 that "its entire archives were kept in a single box in a small [London] hotel room under [a] bed"[138]. The attitude of ultra-Orthodox Judaism was scornful. "According to rabbinic stricture," Segev writes, "God had enjoined the Jews not to 'break the wall,' meaning not to take the land of Israel by force of arms, and not to 'rebel against the nations' who ruled over the Jews. The Jews were to wait for rather than 'push toward the end'—the messianic age in which the land would be restored to the Jews"[139]. A speaker at a Muslim-Christian Association meeting in Jaffa declared, "We do not at all oppose the Jews. We only oppose Zionism. That is not the same thing. Zionism has no roots at all in Moses' law. It is an invention of [Theodor] Herzl's"[140].

An influential Zionist philosopher, Ahad Ha'am, published a pamphlet entitled "Truth from Palestine" in 1891. "The Jewish settlers, he wrote, 'treat the Arabs with hostility and cruelty, trespass unjustly, beat them shamelessly for no sufficient reason, and even take pride in doing so.' He offered a psychological explanation for the phenomenon: 'The Jews were slaves in the land of their Exile, and suddenly they found themselves with unlimited freedom .... This sudden change has produced in their hearts an inclination toward repressive tyranny, as always happens when a slave rules.' [He] warned: 'We are used to thinking of the Arabs as primitive men of the desert, as a donkey-like nation that neither sees nor understands what is going on around it. But this is a great error. The Arab, like all sons of Shem, has a sharp and crafty mind . . . . Should the time come when the life of our people in Palestine imposes to a smaller or greater extent on the natives, they will not easily step aside'"[141].

Population transfer was an essential goal of Zionism from its early years, "a logical outgrowth of the principle of segregation between Jews and Arabs and a reflection of the desire to ground the Jewish state in European, rather than Middle Eastern, culture"[142]. Herzl's diary in June 1895 contains the following sentence: "We shall try to spirit the penniless populations across the border by procuring employment for them in the transit countries, while denying them employment in our own country"[143].

Because of famous writer Israel Zangwill's frank advocacy of transfer in the 1920s, and the widespread criticism it led to, Zionists learned the prudence of concealing their objective in order to retain the world's sympathy[144]. Thus, presumably, little fanfare accompanied the setup of their Committee on Population Transfer in the 1930s. Even those favoring "voluntary" transfer "referred not to the will of the individual but to an agreement between states"[145].

A few years ago the attorney general in the Yitzhak Rabin administration, Michael Ben Yair, wrote in *Ha'aretz*:

> "The Six-Day War was forced on us; but the war's Seventh day, which began on June 12, 1967—continues to this day and is the product of our choice. We enthusiastically chose to become a colonialist society, ignoring international treaties, expropriating lands, transferring settlers from Israel to the occupied territories, engaging in theft and finding justifications for all this"[146].

Menachem Begin, leader of the Etzel terrorist group, wanted 'redemption of the land' by force. His organization's symbol was "a rifle within a map of Palestine reaching to the Iraqi border, and the words ONLY THUS"[147]. On quite a number of occasions this chilling symbol grew shoe leather, as when Etzel operatives in the 1930s "threw bombs into Arab coffeehouses and marketplaces, causing dozens of deaths"[148]. These model citizens financed their terror through bank robbery and extortion[149].

Those who consider the end to justify the means might admire the extent and skill of efforts to organize and carry out evil acts that spread fear not only among Arabs but within the offices and police stations of the British authorities. Lechi, another gang that stood foursquare in the rabbinic tradition, tried twice to assassinate High Commissioner Harold MacMichael and then in November 1944 succeeded in finishing off Lord Moyne, Britain's senior representative in Egypt[150]. Etzel thugs attacked a police station, hanged two British sergeants and, on July 22, 1946, blew up the King David Hotel, wherein the government secretariat had its offices. Ninety-one people lost their lives. In January 1948, Zionists destroyed the Samiramis Hotel, killing many guests and, a few months later, massacred dozens of Arab civilians, women and children among them, in the village of Deir Yassin[151].

Is it any wonder that the Palmachniks, yet another small army of Zionist perps, admired Stalin, or that labor movement leader David Ben-Gurion "compared Begin to the fuehrer"[152]? Raymond Cafferata, Hebron's police chief, described Begin as "a ruthless thug who made Al Capone look like a novice"[153]. Begin would later become the Israeli Prime Minister.

More than half a century later, the nation of Israel continues to break one wall, in violation of rabbinic Judaism, while building another. Force is employed to steal even more land, and the security wall rises higher and grows longer. Farmland is uprooted, aquifer wells commandeered, income sources taken away and lives made miserable by numerous checkpoints where Arabs are humiliated and required to wait hours before being waved through. Trips of 50 miles take 6 hours. Prime Minister Sharon admitted to the Israeli newspaper *Yedioth Ahronoth* that the security wall will end up almost three times longer than the Green Line[154].

Too little of the spirit of Khalil al-Sakakini, a leader of the Arabs during the British Mandate, is in evidence in the Holy Land today. He said: "I hate the Jew when he assaults an Arab and I hate the Arab when he assaults a Jew and I hate all humanity when it is a humanity of hatred and hostility." Sakakini's calling card bore the motto "Human being, God willing"[155]. Wise counsel also came from the lips of early Zionist Chaim Margalit Kalvarisky. "As long as the Jews don't do to the Arabs what they don't want done to themselves by the gentiles in the Diaspora, and so long as they did not build their homes on the ruin of others, there was a chance for détente"[156].

Would that both sides (not to mention the US) would rise to the ethical plane envisioned by Sakakini in his advice to a senior Arab commander on rules of war:

> "the wounded must be cared for, prisoners must be treated properly, soldiers' bodies must be returned. He quoted the words of the first Arab *khalif*: 'Thou shalt not kill a child, an old man, or a woman, thou shalt not burn a tree nor destroy a house, thou shalt not pursue one who flees and thou shalt not mutilate bodies, thou shalt not harm he who is occupied in the worship of God'"[157].

An Arab doctor wrote these words after the Holocaust:

> We all sympathize with the Jews and are shocked at the way Christian nations are persecuting them. But do you expect Moslems of Palestine . . . to be more Christian or more humanitarian than the followers of Christ: Germany, Italy, Poland, Romania, etc. etc.? Have we to suffer in order to make good what you Christians commit"[158]?

Sir Henry Gurney, chief secretary of the Mandate government, pondered on the likely American response had the Jews called for a homeland for themselves in New York[159].

Even when the ancient Israelites were poised to conquer Canaan, the land God had promised them, they behaved presumptuously. They refused to invade in the manner God had prescribed. "Moses said, 'Why are you disobeying the Lord's command? This will not succeed! Do not [attack], because the Lord is not with you. You will be defeated by your enemies, for the Amalekites and Canaanites will face you there. Because you have turned away from the Lord, he will not be with you and you will fall by the sword.' Nevertheless, in their presumption they went up toward the high hill country, though neither Moses nor the ark of the Lord's covenant moved from the camp. Then the Amalekites and Canaanites who lived in that hill country came down and attacked them and beat them down all the way to Hormah" (Numbers 14:41-45). Had they been there, modern Christians would have excitedly pointed out the Israelites moving in for attack and exclaimed reverently, 'Look! Over there! It's the children of the Lord! They're going up to conquer the Promised Land! May God bless them!' But because of their presumption, He didn't.

"But if they will confess their sins and the sins of their fathers—their treachery against me and their hostility toward me, which made me hostile toward them so that I sent them into the land of their enemies—then when their uncircumcised hearts are humbled and they pay for their sin, I will remember my covenant with Jacob and my covenant with Isaac and my covenant with Abraham, and I will remember the land" (Leviticus 26:40-42).

CHAPTER 7

THE MINISTRY OF RECONCILIATION TODAY

"So from now on we regard no one from a worldly point of view. Though we once regarded Christ in this way, we do so no longer. Therefore, if anyone is in Christ, he is a new creation; the old has gone, the new has come! All this is from God, who reconciled us to himself through Christ and gave us the ministry of reconciliation: that God was reconciling the world to himself in Christ, not counting men's sins against them. And he has committed to us the message of reconciliation. We are therefore Christ's ambassadors, as though God were making his appeal through us" (II Corinthians 5:16-20).

What does the Bible mean by the word 'reconciliation'? A commentator considers it a "divine act by which, on the basis of the death of Christ, God's holy displeasure against sinful man was appeased, the enmity between God and man was removed, and man was restored to proper relations with God . . . Reconciliation is not some polite ignoring or reduction of hostility but rather its total and objective removal"[160]. Without wishing to slight the theological aspect of this passage in the least, in this chapter I'll try to map the paradigm of reconciliation onto the current conflict between the United States and the *umma*, the worldwide community of Muslims.

Speaking of the former, most Christian leaders approach the conflict in a spirit of worldliness. "But the wisdom that comes from heaven is first of all pure; then peace-loving, considerate, submissive, full of mercy and good fruit, impartial and sincere. Peacemakers who sow in peace raise a harvest of righteousness" (James 3:17-18). "All her [ie, wisdom's] paths are peace" (Proverbs 3:17). "Live in peace with each other" (I

Thessalonians 5:13). Sadly, the leaders believe in judgment and vengeance instead of mercy (not to mention attacking a nation that's done us no harm), endless war instead of peacemaking, partiality regarding presidential behavior and the Holy Land, hurtful words rather than consideration for others' feelings and lack of submission to God's word while actively encouraging others through violence to rebel against civil authority. But "speak and act as those who are going to be judged by the law that gives freedom, because judgment without mercy will be shown to anyone who has not been merciful. Mercy triumphs over judgment!" (James 2:12-13). The church, not the Republican Party, should be the salt of the earth. Have mercy on Muslims and Bill Clinton!

The November 2002 issue of *Current History* was devoted entirely to political Islam. One pundit therein warns of the risk of "looking through lenses that only see threats and not opportunities" for reconciliation[161]. The same author, P.W. Singer, an Olin Fellow in Foreign Policy Studies at the Brookings Institution and coordinator of the Brookings Project on U.S. Policy Toward the Islamic World, suggests that our government should "encourage and assist moderate voices of reform and tolerance [in Islamic countries] by eliminating the sources of anger that fuel support for radicals"[162].

Please consider the character of God. "I know that the Lord secures justice for the poor and upholds the cause of the needy" (Psalm 140:12). "He upholds the cause of the oppressed and gives food to the hungry. The Lord sets prisoners free, the Lord gives sight to the blind, the Lord lifts up those who are bowed down, the Lord loves the righteous. The Lord watches over the alien and sustains the fatherless and the widow, but he frustrates the ways of the wicked" (Psalm 146:7-9). "The Lord is gracious and compassionate, slow to anger and rich in love. The Lord is good to all; he has compassion on all he has made" (Psalm 145:8-9). "But love your enemies, do good to them . . . . Then your reward will be great, and you will be sons of the Most High, because he is kind to the ungrateful and wicked. Be merciful, just as your Father is merciful" (Luke 6:35-36). "Get rid of all bitterness, rage and anger, brawling and slander, along with every form of malice. Be kind and compassionate to one another, forgiving each other, just as in Christ God forgave you" (Ephesians 4:31-32). If you believe in God, follow in His path.

Archbishop Leighton counsels us to despise no one.

> "The Jews," he wrote, "would not willingly tread upon the smallest piece of paper in their way, but took it up; for possibly, said they, the name of God may be on it. Though there was a little superstition in this, yet truly there is nothing but good religion in it, if we apply it to men. Trample not on any; there may be some work of grace there, that thou knowest not of. The name of God may be written upon that soul thou treadest on; it may be a soul that Christ thought so much of, as to give His precious blood for it; therefore despise it not"[163].

Speak well of others and refrain from calumny.

> "It is [the mark] of a candid ingenuous mind," so say Leighton and Coleridge, "to delight in the good name and commendations of others; to pass by their defects, and take notice of their virtues; and to speak and hear of [the latter] willingly, and not endure either to speak or hear of the [former]; for in this indeed you may be little less guilty than the evil speaker, in taking pleasure in it, though you speak it not. He that willingly drinks in tales and calumnies, will, from the delight he hath in evil hearing, slide insensibly into the [vice] of evil speaking. It is strange how most persons dispense with themselves in this point, and that in scarcely any societies shall we find a hatred of this ill, but rather some tokens of taking pleasure in it; and until a Christian sets himself to an inward watchfulness over his heart, not [allowing] in it any thought that is uncharitable, or vain self-esteem, upon the sight of others' frailties, he will still be subject to somewhat of this, in the tongue or ear at least. So, then, as for the evil of guile in the tongue, a sincere heart, *truth in the inward parts*, powerfully redresses it; therefore it is expressed [in] Psalm 15:2, *That speaketh the truth from his heart*; thence it flows. Seek much after this, [namely] to speak nothing with God, nor men, but what is the sense of a single unfeigned heart. O sweet truth! excellent but rare sincerity!

he that loves that truth within, and who is himself at once
THE TRUTH and THE LIFE, He alone can work it there!
Seek it of him.

It is characteristic of the Roman dignity and sobriety, that, in
the Latin, *to favor with the tongue (favere lingua)* means *to be
silent*. We say, Hold your tongue! as if it were an injunction,
that could not be carried into effect but by manual force, or
the pincers of the Forefinger and Thumb! And [truly]—I blush
to say it—it is not Women and Frenchmen only that would
rather have their tongues bitten than [bridled], and feel their
souls in [confinement], when they are obliged to remain
silent"[164].

According to Augustus Richard Norton, a contributing editor to *Current
History* and a professor of anthropology and international relations at
Boston University, "extensive scientific polling demonstrates that most
Muslims do not hate American values or freedoms"[165]. Riaz Hassan is a
sociologist who was trained at the Punjab and Ohio State Universities.
His book, *Faithlines: Muslim Conceptions of Islam and Society*, compiles the
fascinating results of his attitude research in Egypt, Kazakhstan,
Indonesia and Pakistan where his survey team conducted 4,500 lengthy
interviews with Muslim men and women. A reviewer of the book
concludes that Islam today is not static or anti-Western. "The sense that
everywhere Islam is moving on, if in varying directions, and not just
setting its face against 'modernity,' the West, and internal change, comes
out very strongly"[166].

I wonder why the Islamic world is synonymous in so many American
minds with Stone Age primitivism and backwardness, when the truth is
that

"at the time when Christian Europe was mired in the Dark
Ages, what knowledge it had even of its own roots was
mediated through Arabic translations of Greek manuscripts.
The Muslim world—Damascus, Baghdad, Grenada, Istanbul,
Fustat, Isfahan—was, for about a thousand years, not just the
preeminent civilization in the world, it was, walled and self-

contained and sequestered China aside, the only civilization. 'For many centuries, the world of Islam was in the forefront of human civilization and achievement'" writes Bernard Lewis[167].

And besides, how could we *not* like a people so many of whom are named Al?

The history of Western philosophy cited in chapter 3 makes the following assertion: "It is gradually being realized that a significant part of Western intellectual heritage relies upon the philosophical works of the Islamic world, and that developments in Muslim Spain from the tenth through the twelfth centuries played a major role in the development of Western philosophy"[168].

In the Qur'an, the word *jahiliyya* refers to the ignorance of the pre-Islamic Arabs, but in the twentieth century Muslim revivalists adapted it to describe an atemporal spiritual condition. Although Christianity and Islam differ in important respects, such as the content of scripture, both religions stand against the essence of *jahiliyya* in its adapted form, namely, the "conscious arrogation of God's authority . . . expressed in the simultaneous repudiation of divine rule (*hakimiyya*) and instantiation of human sovereignty. Human sovereignty entails the claim that human beings have the right to establish moral . . . rules for collective behavior, but all such [morals have] already been provided by [scripture] . . . ."[169]

Confusingly, *jahiliyya* is often translated 'modernity,' although there's another meaning of this English word which refers to the intellectual, cultural, commercial and military dominance the West currently enjoys over the rest of the world because of colonialism, imperialism and now globalization[170]. Although it's common for Americans to accept this hegemony uncritically, part of my purpose in writing this book is to spark a thoughtful debate in light of biblical teaching on such matters as the will to dominate, the urge to meddle, the Golden Rule and the importance of peace and humility. I'll employ the term 'modernist juggernaut' to distinguish this usage of the word 'modernity' from the previous one. And those who look favorably on Western hegemony as essentially benign in its effects might find their enthusiasm tempered somewhat after chatting with First Americans or African-Americans or Iraqis. Were you in their shoes, how would you want to be treated?

What Leighton and Coleridge have to say about Christians who differ amongst themselves on points of doctrine can with equal fruitfulness be applied to how those outside the faith are treated.

> "They who have attained to a self-pleasing pitch of civility or formal religion, have usually that point of presumption with it, that they make their own size the model and rule to examine all by. What is below it, they condemn indeed as profane; but what is beyond it, they [consider] needless and affected preciseness; and therefore are as ready as others to let fly invectives or bitter taunts against it, which are the keen and poisoned shafts of the tongue, and a persecution that shall be called to a strict account.

> The slanders, perchance, may not be altogether forged or untrue; they may be the implements, not the inventions, of Malice. But they do not on this account escape the guilt of detraction. Rather, it is characteristic of the evil spirit in question, to work by the advantage of real faults; but these stretched and [exaggerated] to the utmost. IT IS NOT EXPRESSIBLE HOW DEEP A WOUND A TONGUE SHARPENED TO THIS WORK WILL GIVE, WITH NO NOISE AND A VERY LITTLE WORD. This is the true *white* gunpowder, which the dreaming [makers] of silent Mischiefs and insensible Poisons sought for in the Laboratories of Art and Nature, in a World of Good; but which was to be found, in its most destructive form, in *the World of Evil, the Tongue*[171].

An example of wounding slander that no doubt alienated many Muslims was evangelist Franklin Graham's remark that Islam is a violent religion. But his own words will bear witness against himself for he implicitly condemns that which he approves of when perpetrated by the US in Iraq. Is Christianity a violent religion because of the crusades, the pogroms, the medieval burnings at the stake, the massacres of Catholics by Protestants and vice versa, the slaughter of the Indians, the lynchings,

Hiroshima and Nagasaki, the tens of millions of abortions and the unprovoked attack on Iraq?

"We put no stumbling block in anyone's path, so that our ministry will not be discredited" (II Corinthians 6:3). "As was fitting for a fellow worker with God who was acting as an ambassador for Christ, Paul tried to put 'no stumbling block in anyone's path' lest the ministry should incur discredit . . . His concern was that [any accusation] should be totally without foundation, that no 'minister of reconciliation' should be guilty of inconsistent or dishonest conduct, and that no handle be given adversaries who wished to ridicule or malign the gospel"[172]. But we've put hypocrisy, slander and even murder in their path. We pray on our knees on Sunday, as the saying goes, and prey on our neighbors the rest of the week. If Mormons invaded your hometown, torturing and murdering your loved ones, would you be more receptive to Mormonism or less? Will Christians ever confess their sins to Iraqis, or have they imbibed the spirit of hatred, arrogance and destructive slander pouring forth from the White House? Who will play God and whack *our* country? Humble introspection seems in short supply. Again, who is salting whom?

A Turk named Said Nursi (1876-1920) inspired the formation of his country's largest social organization, the Nur movement, which promotes Islamic values while eschewing political activism and violence. As a matter of principle, they make no attempt to take over the government or implement *sharia* (Islamic law)[173]. Could the Christian right learn anything from them about political quietism, or are we quick to speak but slow to listen? Muhiddin Kabiri, the clean-shaven and jeans-clad deputy chairman of Tajikistan's Islamic Revival Party, stresses that setting up a theocratic state is not a party goal at all. "The IRP—still the only legal religious party in [Central Asia]—has kept its promise to stick to democratic rules" and its priority continues to be "maintaining stability in the country"[174].

In a Survey of Islam and the West, an analyst writes that "it seems obvious that unless the moderate Islamists are given a fair hearing, disaffected citizens [of Muslim countries] will turn to the violent organizations on their fringes which, since Iraq and Afghanistan, have a potent message of global Muslim beleaguerment to recruit more followers." The same writer warns us not to meddle in an internal Muslim debate. "[America] should beware of stepping into somebody else's argument about the true meaning of Islam, and of assuming that democracy must be Islam's opposite. These are arguments for Muslims to resolve, in their own way"[175]. After all, we wouldn't appreciate it one bit if Muslims intervened in our religious debates. "Make it your ambition to lead a quiet life, to mind your own business . . . so that your daily life may win the respect of outsiders" (I Thessalonians 4:11-12).

Please keep in mind that part of the reason for increased Muslim activism in recent years is us. We officially support many of the Muslim regimes although most of them are corrupt and oppressive failures; and our bias in the Arab-Israeli conflict prompted one wag to dub Capitol Hill Israeli-occupied territory[176]. "[Muslim citizens'] resentment is with an existing political order, supported by the United States, that they cannot affect." As Israel continues to increase the number of settlers in the West Bank, we continue to help financially and politically, and Muslims grow more and more alienated from us[177]. Pro-Israel Christians are also an obstacle to peace because they refuse to see the 1948 dispossession of the Palestinians as evil. As presidents favor the evangelicals who favor Israel, "even more poisoned feeling between the Arabs and the United States" will ensue[178]. But the Apostle Paul says: "I charge you, in the sight of God and Christ Jesus and the elect angels, to keep these instructions without partiality, and to do nothing out of favoritism" (I Timothy 5:21). Perhaps one way to reduce Muslim alienation (another way will be broached at the end of this chapter) is to reverse our longstanding support of failed Muslim states and press for democratization[179].

As a remedy for our pride, whether in ourselves individually or in our country or if we preen as we glance disdainfully at the Muslim *umma*, here is a pithy offering from Leighton:

> "Too many take the ready course to deceive themselves; for they look with both eyes on the failings and defects of others, and scarcely give their good qualities half an eye, while on the contrary, in themselves, they study to the full their own advantages, [whereas] their weaknesses and defects (as one says) they skip over, as children do their hard words in their lesson, that are troublesome to read; and making this uneven

parallel, what wonder if the result be a gross mistake of themselves"[180]!

Too much of Americans' hatred and fear of Islam stems from ignorance of its content, denial of the skeletons in our own closet, and displacement or projection of our primitive or irrational or tribalistic impulses onto the Other. Wasn't it tribalistic to murder African-Americans by lynch mob and race riot? Isn't it primitive to keep severed testicles from a lynch victim as souvenirs? Isn't it irrational to hate our victims intensely for centuries? In an essay that sheds much light not only on jihad but on "the larger phenomenon of killing or dying for politics"[181], Roxanne Euben, a political science professor at Wellesley College, writes that

> "given the violence and coercion so often undertaken in the name of democracy, it is difficult to regard attempts to make jihad the sole repository of bloody-minded impulses as anything other than the displacement of anxieties about killing and dying for politics onto an Islamic other. Such displacement, in turn, depends on flattened (mis)understandings of a variety of non-Western thought and practices and on the other, hidden [ie, suppressed] histories within the . . . West in which death (often violent) is implicated in both the creation and continued existence of even the democratic public realm"[182].

How to rid ourselves of doublemindedness, this confident condemnation in others of what we excuse in our own case?

> "All true remedy must begin at the heart; otherwise it will be but a mountebank cure, a false imagined conquest. The weights and wheels are *there*, and the clock strikes according to their motion. Even he that speaks contrary to what is within him, guilefully contrary to his inward conviction and knowledge, yet speaks conformably to what is within him in the temper and frame of his heart, which is double, *a heart and a heart*, as the Psalmist hath it (Psalm 12:2)"[183]

Here's some food for thought. If you live in the West but devoutly follow a Middle Eastern religion like Judaism, Christianity or Islam, are you truly a Westerner? Categories such as East and West are too often conceived of as if they're distinct, impenetrable physical objects, rather like billiard balls that bounce away from each other after a collision. But more fruitful—not to mention, honest—is to think of East and West as spirits that interpenetrate upon contact (provided we remember that, as in the case of, say, a spirit of friendship or a spirit of humility, they possess no will or personality). Boundaries between cultures are porous and "identities in a postcolonial and now globalized world are relational, permeable, and culturally syncretic"[184]. As a follower of Christ, the One who revealed Himself to us in a book written mostly in the East, how could I honestly claim to be nothing but a Westerner, instead of drawing inspiration from He who showers compassion on all He has made?

> Besides, "the sheer number of Muslims living as minorities in non-Muslim countries makes a nonsense of the simple notion that Islam and the West comprise separate geopolitical power blocks doomed to collide. Almost one in three of the world's Muslims (if you include the 133 million in India alone) lives in a country where Muslims are a minority . . . Muslims in the West, or in India, [hence] have a powerful vested interest of their own in the safety, prosperity and continued tolerance of the non-Islamic societies in which they live"[185].

Not only are Westerners (so-called Westerners, that is) influenced by the East, but conversely Easterners partake of the spirit of the West. A Muslim intellectual based in the US, Abdullahi an-Naim, expresses profound skepticism about the implementation of Islamic law. He writes that the "public law of Shari'a is fundamentally inconsistent with the realities of modern life. This is my firm conviction as a Muslim. My only concern is to avoid the human suffering which is likely to be caused by this doomed endeavor"[186]. And about a century ago, another influential Muslim reformer, Jamal al-Din al-Afghani, tried to adapt Western ideas and institutions to Muslim sensibilities and values. Even to this day, "the al-Afghani Society, which brings together hundreds of Egyptian intellectuals and professionals, meets periodically in Cairo"[187].

The use of the term *jihad* is sometimes, whether intentionally or not, deceptive when its meaning is distorted due to ignorance of its history or when it's employed as an emotive code word to project our wickedness onto neighbors[188] who've become our enemies largely because of our aggressive and murderous hypocrisy. (In the past few years, we've whacked two of their countries, but how many non-Muslim states have they conquered in the last three centuries?)

The meaning of *jihad* has evolved over time and retains some ambiguity regarding the use of force. According to an Arabic-English dictionary, it means "'exerting one's utmost power, efforts, endeavors, or ability in contending with an object of disapprobation' or striving toward a worthy goal"[189]. Those who argue that jihad is a non-violent idea point to the passage in the Qur'an (2:256) that "there is no compulsion in religion." And another verse says "Hold back your hands (from attacking), observe your devotional obligations and pay the *zakat* [alms]" (4:77). Some nineteenth century Muslim thinkers, including the Indian Sayyid Ahmad Khan and Egyptians Muhammad Abduh and Rashid Rida, argued that "peace, rather than enmity, was the normative state of affairs between Muslims and non-Muslims"[190]. And a contemporary, Khalil Abdel Alim of the American Muslim Mission, declares that "jihad does not mean fighting a war; it means struggle for what is required of one in obedience to God . . . Getting out of bed for dawn prayer . . . is jihad"[191].

On the other hand, there are those who employ jihad as a rationale for violence against what I've referred to as the 'modernist juggernaut'. Two prominent advocates of this approach were the Pakistani Mawlana Abu al-Ala Mawdudi (1903-1979) and Egypt's Sayyid Qutb (1906-1966), both of whom regarded the expansionist ambitions of the juggernaut as "a justification for a 'permanent revolution' where fine distinctions between defensive and offensive jihad have little meaning"[192]. Earlier in Islam's history, their jurists developed a "coherent doctrine that legitimized force in defense and expansion of Islam and linked the pursuit of jihad to the realization of justice within a concrete social order, obedience to divine guidance, and the 'desire to secure the well-being of all humanity'"[193]. But from the tenth century onwards, this doctrine of expansionist jihad "assumed a dormant status'[194]. Mawdudi and Qutb represented a sea change in conceptualization, according to the author Emmanuel Sivan, in pushing for jihad *within* the *umma* against governments perceived as illegitimate because they aided the juggernaut while betraying Islam. Indeed, the assistance was part of the betrayal[195].

Christians can play a vital role in making peace today in two ways: first, by refusing to support unjust or oppressive governments at home or abroad; and second, by humbly offering another perspective on the nexus between killing and politics, one that, sadly, hasn't been put into practice yet by a nation conceived in covetousness and godless revolt, dedicated to the proposition that all Property-Owning Male Protestant Anglo-Saxons (POMPAS) are created equal, and founding what remained—at least for a while—a government of the POMPAS, by the people (forget not the Revolutionary War Full Moon Gang, the elite's thuggish enforcement arm) and for the POMPAS.

First, begin with the distinction between church and state. In the words of Bernard Lewis, "Throughout the history of Christendom there have been two powers: God and Caesar . . . . always there are two, with its [sic] own laws and jurisdictions, its own structure and hierarchy"[196].

Second, note the state's monopoly on violence in the Romans 13:1ff. passage cited in chapter 1. (The most severe punishment imposed by the New Testament church was excommunication).

Third, I reiterate the Bible's emphasis on peacemaking, pursuing peace, and leading a quiet life.

Fourth, I call your attention to what Hannah Arendt calls "the triumph of the eternal over the immortal" with the advent of Christianity, when

> "the ancient emphasis on earthly and collective immortality was displaced by the preoccupation with the eternal life of the human individual . . . [Thus] human existence becomes the highest good. This is so not because of any lasting significance to worldly events and human actions, but because simple existence is the [last] step [before] eternal life"[197].

Fifth, according to Arendt's essay "[p]olitical activity, which until then had derived its greatest inspiration from the striving toward worldly immortality, now sank to the low level of an activity subject to necessity, destined to remedy the consequences of human sinfulness and to cater to the legitimate wants and interests of earthly life"[198].

Sixth, wait for God to bring to justice those who sin against us. Nelson Mandela forgave the apartheid regime! Why act godlessly? Who would Jesus bomb? God will inaugurate the Golden Age of heaven on earth, too. Don't do His work for Him. Wait for Him!

Seventh, confess our sins and those of our fathers to God and to those we've wronged—including the juggernaut's violence and aggressive expansion—and then repent.

Sadly, a "'legacy of violence' is part of the paradox of political foundings, an inheritance at once denied and omnipresent in the ongoing existence of even the democratic territorial state"[199]. Machiavelli suggested "not that all politics is violent, but that the violence of a founding may be the precondition to politics at all"[200].

A statesmanlike response to the September 11th attacks would've been:

1.) a humble apology to the world for all our innocent bloodshed, because the same standard we hold others to will be used by God to judge us (Matthew 7:2);
2.) the Israeli government would be required to remove all settlers from the Occupied Territories within six months;
3.) a truth and reconciliation commission, chaired by Norway or some other neutral party, would be established to collect evidence of, and grant restitution for, documented cases of Israeli crimes against Palestinians since 1948, provided the victims permanently surrender the right of return to Israel proper.

CHAPTER 8

TWICE MORE INTO THE BREACH

The Story of King Shin

"Don't you know Taanach?" asked the grinning King Shin, Big Cheese of the informal Kingdom of Kanah, of the approaching supplicant.

"Nope, never met him." Loud boisterous guffaws filled the audience hall from the direction of a small crowd performing the role of something like a Greek chorus. Cheerily one of them called out to the old man now kneeling before the throne: "And how do we always greet our king?"

"Wadi yahsadad?"

"Hey, old man," cried Shin. The chorus waited expectantly for the usual greeting for an oldie. "Gezer." Loud laughter pealed forth again while Shin grinned appreciatively. "Let's see," he added thoughtfully, studying his notes, "are you here about the lion that let out Aroer?"

"No, sire."

"What's your name then?" he asked, puzzled.

"Nippur." Royal advisor Bene Rabud whispered "Nippur of Tadmor."

"Ah yes, now I remember. The town drunk." Nippur blushed and studied the rug intently. "So what's new with you, Nippie?" he added breezily.

"It's about Berothai again, sire," he blurted out shamefacedly.

The king frowned. "Been messing with those hormahs again?" he asked, a trifle ominously. Murmurs of disapproval from the royal chorus. "What about your poor wife?"

Shocked by the question, Nippur gazed into the eyes of the king, but saw no hint of levity. Had he forgotten? But then possibly he had! The old man glanced at the face of Bajarim, he of the royal retinue, who'd just then stepped forward in front of Shin, the barest hint of swagger in his carriage. Nippur bitterly recalled the plight of his beloved late wife. She'd been overheard in the town square complaining about an injury. "What am I going to do about that shin?" she asked a friend. A sense of unease gripped his heart when he noticed Bajarim, jaw jutting forward, closely watching his face for signs of discontent. The retainer glanced back at Shin and nodded. As Nippur was being escorted—if that's the word—from the audience hall, he cried out plaintively, "But—but what about Berothai? She stole all my money in my sleep!"

Playing their role of mood shifter to perfection (at other times they merely echoed it), the chorus began to chant "Story! story! story!," building to a crescendo whereupon, at a signal of assent from the king, cheers and applause resounded. Shin snapped his fingers and a servant materialized—poof!—just like that.

"Ascus."

"Yes, sire?"

"Two cold drinks."

"Two, sire?" came the jocular reply. The king playfully knocked the servant's head gear off. Chuckles from the peanut gallery. Quicker than a fleet-footed lizard disappears from a darkened room when the door's opened wide, the refreshments were handed off. Shin gave one to Bajarim who, as he doted on his leader, was visibly moved by this sign of special favor.

"Ascus."

"Sire?" It was a different servant this time, but no matter. All of them bore this name. (Wasn't a certain Syrian town founded by a stranded traveling merchant whose servant stole all his worldly goods, his mules, even his faithful wife and lovely daughters, and was never heard from again? Not even so much as a lousy letter from the no-good ingrate! But let that pass for now).

"This isn't sweet enough." Moments later, when he'd gotten situated, he began his life story thusly: "Long, long ago, in the village of Ibleam-Meneba, dear old Ma, who wasn't so old *then*, sensed that it was time. They say it was sunny and windy the day I was born, so windy in fact that the few puffy clouds, the shape and color of handfuls of clumpy cotton, scooted right on across the sky and got teeny-weeny and disappeared in practically no time at all. My squalls—didn't care for that slap across the fanny, mind you—scared a rabbit under the window that suddenly, in a flash, moved off onto the road quicker than lightning, which ended up spooking a Hee-Haw that consequently sounded off, which happens a lot when they're stressed, so a passerby says to the poor critter "pipe down" which offended a young Casanova making romantic small talk with his lass, so he turns and punches the guy right in the honker but, being tough, he recovered in no time and caved a ceramic jar over Romeo's noggin who, wonder of wonders, somehow had the presence of mind to pick up the jar handle and bean the guy so hard that, naturally, things escalated and got out of hand. The poor heartbroken young lady cried buckets at the funeral which of course I didn't know at the time seeing as how I was busy stuffing things into my mouth and peeing on anyone dumb enough to get into range whenever I was ready to let 'er rip. If you ask me, not that you *have*, I say it was all the apple juice they gave me. It was apple juice for this and apple juice for that. When I cried, they gave me apple juice. When I quit crying, they rewarded me with apple juice. Apple juice at wakey-wakey time, and apple juice at beddie-bye, not to mention nappie time and din-din. I got so sick of the stuff and so tired of all the urinating that I stomped my lil' feet up and down rapidly and bellered but they tried to calm me down with—you guessed it."

The king paused reflectively and let out a heavy sigh. It was only then that he noticed his surroundings. Literally everyone in the hall, even the chorus, was sound asleep, many of them snoring peacefully. Servants sat back motionless against the wall, advisors lovingly hugged throne legs, one of them (was it Bajarim?) hugged the royal brogans, soldiers curled up on the floor neatly inside their shields. There was even a lizard sprawled in the middle of the floor that'd sensed an opportunity to take a shortcut but succumbed on the way. Its head rested comfortably on a paw while the other three splayed out all around. A roach, a fly and a flea slept fitfully between the spines on its back. One catches a few winks whenever and wherever one can.

Shin surveyed the touching scene, grinning like a jackass eating briers. His eye rested on Bene Rabud's troubled face. Buddie seemed to be having a bad dream. Listening closely, Shin thought he could make out the words "You da man, you da man." Two old biddies were shopping for veggies. Ukiah the Hippi (pron. HIP-eye) mourned for her late husband Tokhath. She went on and on about all the ways she missed him while her friend Bathshivah listened so sympathetically that tears stood in her eyes. (She always shivered when stepping out of her bath and hence her nickname, which she minded not one whit as her given name had been Choga Mami). She gently steered the conversation towards the subject of eligible replacements for Tokhath, but Ukiah, pouring scorn on the local men, would have nothing to do with such a prospect. This led, quite naturally in the latter's eyes, to talk about animals and then on to the subject of roaches, one or two of which lurked among the tomatoes they were inspecting at the moment. Ukiah picked up a tomato to test for firmness but found it squishy. "Rotten", she observed caustically. While in the air a roach on the underside lost his grip and fell onto her robe. Frantically she cried out "It's on my SHIN! Kill him!!" When the king was informed, she found herself arrested and tortured. She later died in prison, supposedly of natural causes, or so they say. Buddie shouted in his dream "You are the man! You are the man!!"

The sound of his voice awakened everyone in the hall. Bajarim instantly sprang to his feet and squared off between Buddie and Shin. His face began to twitch uncontrollably. The cat Begonia's body stretched, forming a backwards upturned C behind the throne. (You have no idea how quickly the lizard and crew disappeared). Invoking Wo, the hoary old god of wrath, he repeated the deity's name 10 or 12 times in rapid succession while glaring intently at Buddie, ready to pounce on anything he said. His face grew even more contorted as if his head would explode. Fiercely indignant, he questioned motives but contemptuously interrupted every attempt to answer his own loaded questions. The king's defender showed no concern whatsoever for how wounding his slanderous accusations were.

"A-C-C-H-O!"

"Haluzah" came the royal response.

"Thanks" said Bajarim as he wiped his nose.

"Don't mention it. Now get back to interrogating Stinkbug." And so, despite years of faithful service to his king, Bene Rabud was unceremoniously fired the next day and replaced with a sycophant. Arrogance and tyranny trump truth and justice, but only for a time.

The Yeast of the Pharisees

Saddam Hussein wearily sorted through his official papers to organize them for his captors while brooding bitterly about the turn his life had taken in December 2003. Suddenly he sat bolt upright, mouth agape, eyes bugging out. Shocked at what he'd just discovered, he let rip a colorful streak of Tikritian profanity that awakened a guard asleep in a chair nearby. Was it CIA disinformation? Evidence of Shiite perfidy? Proof of a trusted lackey's betrayal? No, it was none of these. Seems that an important news bulletin of his supposed to have been aired by the Ministry of Information decades ago had fallen through the cracks.

During a hastily arranged press conference that he insisted on, he announced to the world's press that, due to a bureaucratic snafu, the following declaration of his was becoming public about 20 years after the fact. Based on information he was unwilling to share, he'd decided after careful thought that all opponents of his regime, both domestic and foreign, were nothing but unlawful combatants.

An aide whispered the news to Pres. Bush during a meeting of his cabinet, whereupon his face grew cloudy and confused for a brief moment. For how was he to interpret this? Was Saddam sincere? Did he honestly feel this way about his enemies? Or was he mocking the leader of the free world? Would Saddam now huffily point out that we all know aggression is self-defense so lay off me about the mass graves? Would he robustly defend the gassing of the Kurds for the same reason, adding tartly that the normal rules don't apply on account of Halabja not being under his control at the time? Indeed the very thing he was trying to accomplish was to regain control! And what if Saddam knew his secret about torture? Bush's face grew hot and beet red as he exploded with rage. He issued an order.

Soon the dastardly prisoner found himself hustled onto a chopper and ferried to downtown Belgrade, where he was unceremoniously shoved off in a park. The chopper quickly disappeared over the horizon only to return moments later. The gunner dropped a paper sack onto the grass and then the pilot sped away for good. When Saddam opened it he found a Serbo-Croatian phrasebook, a dog-eared issue of Texas Ranger magazine and a glazed donut. Bush ordered his entire administration never to speak to Hussein again.

The President lay tossing and turning in bed, sweating profusely and crying "No! no! no!" His wife caressed him with comforting words. Had it been only a dream? Quickly he turned on the news but saw nothing out of the ordinary, unless you count a few veiled references to The Incident in Belgrade, whatever that meant.

But his relief—if you can call it that—turned to unease when someone from Capitol Hill called him about the herd of Democrats laughing uproariously while huddling around a certain TV broadcast from Serbia. For it seems that Hussein was performing in a celebrity roast before an audience of retired Serbian mafiosi with bulging upper torsos and low-brimmed fedoras. The erstwhile dictator sported the toga and sandals and olive wreath of a Roman emperor. When a succession of handcuffed prisoners bowed before him one by one he cocked his head thoughtfully and whispered questions to an attendant about each one. He would sometimes ponder for a while, then shrug his shoulders and give the thumbs up, in which case the grateful prisoner would be released and fly weeping into the arms of his next of kin.

But alas for the others, defeated and destroyed by a down-turned thumb! Often for them fate frowned in the form of a cleaning lady who diffidently swept her way up to a certain man of lawlessness and timidly spoke rumors into his ear at close range while he nodded, glaring darkly down at the helpless man.

CHAPTER 9

WHY I LEFT THE REPUBLICAN PARTY

A lifelong Republican, son of a John Birch Republican father, I left the party in 1999 because of injustice, hypocrisy and deceit.

Suppose a Muslim-American were arrested on a false charge of DUI and that during the pre-trial phase the prosecutor came to the conclusion that the defendant was innocent. But instead of dropping the charge, the prosecutor decides to try for a charge of perjury by asking the defendant under oath, Do you believe in God? This line of questioning is itself an obstruction of justice because justice requires the speedy acquittal of the innocent. The trial is not about religion, but whether or not the crime of DUI was committed. If the defendant is innocent of the charge, then his worship of Allah or Krishna or Money or wax fruit is irrelevant.

Also please note the question's ambiguity. The question 'Are you a Muslim?' is clear, but 'Do you believe in God?' isn't. What does the questioner mean by 'God'?

Unaware of the machinations of Republican justice, our hapless defendant answers the question truthfully. Yes, he says, I believe in God. And thus—without an indictment—he's accused of perjury because, supposedly, everyone knows that the word 'God' means 'Jehovah'. But what matters is whether the defendant intended to deceive and whether his response materially affected the trial's outcome. And remember that the outcome should've been an acquittal prior to asking the question about God. If the defendant in a humorous aside mentioned that he'd just returned from the bathroom where he'd discovered that he was actually a woman, clearly this is not perjury because intent to deceive was absent and because his gender has no bearing on the case.

Likewise, during Bill Clinton's sexual harassment trial, what mattered was whether he sexually harassed the plaintiff, Paula Jones. The reason the judge ruled in January 1998 that any information about the President's relationship with Monica Lewinsky was inadmissible was that the former didn't harass the latter. Thus the question whether he had sex with her obstructs justice in deflecting attention from the Jones case—why not just ask him whether he had sex with his wife?!—and is ambiguous because of the word 'sex'. And forget not that the Jones case was later dismissed because it had no merit, according to the judge.

Sometimes it seemed to me that Republicans yearned to chuck American jurisprudence out the window and replace it with a simple three-step process: accusation, confession and punishment. But had you been on trial, how would you've wanted to be treated?

"The ruthless will vanish, the mockers will disappear, and all who have an eye for evil will be cut down—those who with a word make a man out to be guilty, who ensnare the defender in court and with false testimony deprive the innocent of justice" (Isaiah 29:20-21).

The hypocrisy of the Clinton bashers is deeply offensive. Suppose they'd trumpeted the rule of law and the importance of justice during Al Capone's day. Suppose Capone murdered, say, 500 people but in the middle of this bloodletting he receives a draft notice. So he joins the army and serves honorably until his term is over. Then it's back to his life of crime, not only whacking victims but obstructing justice in each and every murder trial by murdering judges or witnesses, intimidation or bribery. Consequently he's guilty of at least 1,000 crimes (500-plus murders and 500 cases of obstruction of justice). Would someone who cared deeply about justice and the rule of law acquiesce quietly to charging Capone with draft evasion but never charging him with any of the 1,000-plus crimes?

Why did Republicans let Ken Starr get away with spending 5 years and $50 million investigating Clinton and then only charge him (falsely) with sexual harassment of Paula Jones and nothing else? Why didn't they go ballistic and insist that obstruction charges be brought on at least a handful of the Whitewater, Travelgate or other allegations? Even if so-called 'Slick Willie' was able to finesse his way out of the underlying charges, there's still the issue of obstruction in doing so. And yet although he was never convicted for any crime, he's still mocked and demonized today. No to concealing fellatio! But yes to character assassination and brazen murder!!

And thus we arrive at the sin of Republican deceit. How is it that a man so thoroughly investigated by unfriendly lawyers but never charged credibly for any crime has become a byword for moral turpitude? And then there's the issue of what I call House Trial Manager Language (HTML). Did they get away with twisting the meanings of words like 'sex' (coitus) into activities that included snapping bra straps? Was 'perjury' (intentional material deception) turned into 'concealing an irrelevant embarrassment'? Was 'obstruction of justice' (thwarting a legal proceeding to escape punishment) reworked to include gathering information calmly from a secretary to ensure that a side issue within a meritless lawsuit would not be mischaracterized, all the while these white-hatted Trial Managers obstructed justice themselves with extensive questioning that delayed acquittal? Yes, they did get away with these evil acts and Republicans applauded them.

If the Party humbly ate crow about the impeachment and trial of Bill Clinton, dousing and throwing away the red-hot shaft of Republican justice, and admitted wrongdoing in invading Iraq in 2003, I'd return to it. Otherwise, I'll become a Republican again only when there's enough white frost in hell to freeze snapbeans.

CHAPTER 10

CONCLUDING SPIRITUAL SUBTEXT

You might find this difficult to believe, but I like my country. I'm not crazy about it, you understand, but I do like it. For this reason, a worldwide Muslim caliphate isn't something I'd want us to become a province of. Like the average teenager, we believe we're nine feet tall and bulletproof. But this supposedly invincible nation was dealt a truly devastating blow on September 11th by just 19 people. Consider what could happen if 10,000-50,000 of the more than one billion Muslims were to attack us. Are we going to be the first great power in world history to last forever? "Pride goes before destruction, a haughty spirit before a fall" (Proverbs 16:18). Perhaps harshness and brutality would imperil our existence as an independent political entity if carried on too long. How to avoid such a chilling outcome forms part of my subtext.

Are you tuned in to the Spirit of the Age, gentle reader? Alas, too often the *Zeitgeist* trivializes the serious but elevates the unimportant. Hell is not peopled solely by serial killers and those who spend an inordinate amount of time alone with live poultry or sheep. The soundtrack down there doesn't blare an endless loop of songs by Tears for Fears (eg, "Everybody Wants to Rule the World," "Shout," "Head Over Heels); Bachman Turner Overdrive ("Ain't Seen Nothin' Yet," "Let It Ride," "Taking Care of Business"); Captain and Tennille (how about "Muskrat Love"?); John Mellencamp ("Small Town"); Leo Sayer ("When I Need Love"); "Love Among the Pallets" by Melvin Weems and the Scanners[201]; anything by Rick Astley and Belinda Carlisle; interspersed with those hard rock-sounding infomercials for muscle toning equipment while the inmates occasionally mop a brow or stifle the odd yawn behind a hand. Those who imagine it that way are sadly mistaken. The unrepentant "murderers, idolaters and everyone who loves and practices falsehood" (Revelation 22:15) will face their destiny of endless "weeping there and gnashing of teeth" (Luke 13:28).

But those who repent and turn toward God to follow His voice make room in their hearts for His word. They don't allow other voices to crowd His out. He says "This is the one I esteem: he who is humble and contrite in spirit, and trembles at my word" (Isaiah 66:2). "'Both prophet and priest are godless; even in my temple I find their wickedness,' declares the Lord. 'They strengthen the hands of evildoers, so that no one turns from his wickedness. But if they had stood in my council, they would have proclaimed my words to my people and would have turned them from their evil ways and from their evil deeds'" (Jeremiah 23:11,14,22). "If anyone turns a deaf ear to the law, even his prayers are detestable" (Proverbs 28:9).

"Once, having been asked by the Pharisees when the kingdom of God would come, Jesus replied, 'The kingdom of God does not come visibly, nor will people say, 'Here it is,' or 'There it is,' because the kingdom of God is within you'" (Luke 17:20-21). A Christian's warfare is not physical but spiritual as the following passage clearly demonstrates: "For our struggle [jihad] is not against flesh and blood, but against the rulers, against the authorities, against the powers of this dark world and against the spiritual forces of evil in the heavenly realms. Therefore put on the full armor of God, so that when the day of evil comes, you may be able to stand your ground, and after you have done everything, to stand. Stand firm then, with the belt of truth buckled around your waist, with the breastplate of righteousness in place, and with your feet fitted with the readiness that comes from the gospel of peace. In addition to all this, take up the shield of faith, with which you can extinguish all the flaming arrows of the evil one. Take the helmet of salvation and the sword of the Spirit, which is the word of God. And pray in the Spirit on all occasions with all kinds of prayers and requests" (Ephesians 6:12-18). There's not even a hint of violence here.

How could the gospel of peace be furthered by strengthening the hand of any politician of any party who favored murder of any kind? We would never countenance the furtherance of Islam through violence, would we? How can Christians influence the country in a good way by promoting innocent bloodshed, hatred, arrogance, slander and divisiveness? Do Christians cling so tightly to their political power that they're deaf to God's voice? The Apostle John says, "Then I heard another voice from heaven say: 'Come out of [Babylon], my people, so that you will not share in her sins'" (Revelation 18:4). Voting for any presidential candidate who supports murder or the right to choose murder sends two powerful messages to the dominant culture: first, that power trumps principle and second, that the bloodiest century in world history, demonstrating the same amoral spirit, taught us nothing whatsoever. Those who replace the all-powerful Prince of Peace with the idol of influence will reap troubles and fears, the bitter fruit of all idolatry. "Those who cling to worthless idols forfeit the grace that could be theirs" (Jonah 2:8).

"When a man's ways are pleasing to the Lord, he makes even his enemies live at peace with him" (Proverbs 16:7). "Whoever corrects a mocker brings on insult; whoever rebukes a wicked man incurs abuse. Do not rebuke a mocker or he will hate you; rebuke a wise man and he will love you. Instruct a wise man and he will be wiser still; teach a righteous man and he will add to his learning" (Proverbs 9:7-9). "A perverse man stirs up dissension (Proverbs 16:28). "The Lord detests men of perverse heart" (Proverbs 11:20). "It is to a man's honor to avoid strife, but every fool is quick to quarrel" (Proverbs 20:3). "There are six things the Lord hates, seven that are detestable to him: haughty eyes, a lying tongue, hands that shed innocent blood, a heart that devises wicked schemes, feet that are quick to rush into evil, a false witness who pours out lies and a man who stirs up dissension among brothers" (Proverbs 6:16-19). "You are not a God who takes pleasure in evil; with you the wicked cannot dwell. The arrogant cannot stand in your presence; you hate all who do wrong. You destroy those who tell lies; bloodthirsty and deceitful men the Lord abhors" (Psalm 5:4-6). "Woe to them! They have taken the way of Cain" (Jude 11). "Whoever loves discipline loves knowledge, but he who hates correction is stupid" (Proverbs 12:1). "Warn a divisive person once, and then warn him a second time. After that, have nothing to do with him. You may be sure that such a man is warped and sinful; he is self-condemned" (Titus 3:10-11). "A man is praised according to his wisdom, but men with warped minds are despised" (Proverbs 12:8). "A wicked man listens to evil lips; a liar pays attention to a malicious tongue" (Proverbs 17:4). "There is deceit in the hearts of those who plot evil, but joy for those who promote peace" (Proverbs 12:20). "These also are sayings of the wise:

To show partiality in judging is not good: Whoever says to the guilty, 'You are innocent'—peoples will curse him and nations denounce him. But it will go well with those who convict the guilty, and rich blessing will come upon them" (Proverbs 24:23-25). "For in his own eyes he flatters himself too much to detect or hate his sin. The words of his mouth are wicked and deceitful; he has ceased to be wise and to do good. Even on his bed he plots evil; he commits himself to a sinful course and does not reject what is wrong" (Psalm 36:2-4). "One who is slack in his work is brother to one who destroys" (Proverbs 18:9). "The kindest acts of the wicked are cruel" (Proverbs 12:10). When Ronald Reagan, that champion of liberty, wasn't looking, US citizens lost a cherished right by another president's fiat and intimidation, a right taken for granted even in ancient Rome: "I told them that it is not the Roman custom to hand over any man [for punishment] before he has faced his accusers and has had an opportunity to defend himself against their charges" (Acts 25:16). "But now I am writing you that you must not associate with anyone who calls himself a brother but is . . . a slanderer . . . . With such a man do not even eat" (I Corinthians 5:11).

What will you do? Will you pledge allegiance to the Spirit of the Age that magnifies the marginal (political influence, say) while trivializing the transcendent voice of God? Has caring for the interests of a politician desensitized your conscience? Do you pledge allegiance to 'one nation under wrath,' loaded down with many unconfessed sins unrepented of, or will you look to the One who brings reconciliation and healing to our land? We Christians chose not to salt the earth after 9/11 but drank in the worldly spirit of passionate vengeance and reckless adventurism. But "it is not good to have zeal without knowledge, nor to be hasty and miss the way" (Proverbs 19:2). "If you suffer, it should not be as a murderer or thief or any other kind of criminal, or even as a meddler" (I Peter 4:15) in another nation's affairs. "Like one who seizes a dog by the ears is a passer-by who meddles in a quarrel not his own" (Proverbs 26:17).

But ignoring these words of wisdom, America intervened in Iraq uninvited after decades of biased intervention in the Holy Land. Why is there so little sympathy in our hearts for Palestinian Christians, the unsung heroes of the Middle East, but we bleed—literally—for their oppressors? "Be alert and always keep on praying for all the saints" (Ephesians 6:18). "Speak up for those who cannot speak for themselves, for the rights of all who are destitute. Speak up and judge fairly; defend the rights of the poor and needy" (Proverbs 31:8-9). "'He defended the cause of the poor and needy, and so all went well. Is that not what it means to know me?' declares the Lord. 'But your eyes and your heart are set only on . . . shedding innocent blood and on oppression'" (Jeremiah 22:16-17). How can reconciliation be achieved without confession of sin, of Zionist sins against Palestinians in the 1930s and 1940s and beyond, of whites' sins against the first Americans and African-Americans, of Northern sins against the South and vice versa, and of our sins against the Muslims?

Why also the unreasoning animus against another victim, Bill Clinton, he who's more sinned against than sinning?

> My mind, because the minds that I have loved,
> The sort of beauty that I have approved,
> Prosper but little, has dried up of late,
> Yet knows that to be choked with hate
> May well be of all evil chances chief.
> If there's no hatred in a mind
> Assault and battery of the wind
> Can never tear the linnet[202] from the leaf.
>
> An intellectual hatred is the worst,
> So let her think opinions are accursed.
> Have I not seen the loveliest woman born
> Out of the mouth of Plenty's horn,
> Because of her opinionated mind
> Barter that horn and every good
> By quiet natures understood
> For an old bellows full of angry wind?

Yeats, *A Prayer for My Daughter*

Clinton's hated for failings we overlook in our friends. Congressman Henry Hyde showed skill in hiding an extramarital affair for years. Bob Barr succeeded in barring a nosy divorce court from prying into details of certain late-night meetings with a warm, close, personal friend to whom he wasn't married. Another Georgia politician accustomed himself to shedding wives—

including one fighting ovarian cancer—like a trotting youngster handles clothing nearing a swimming hole. Mayor Rudy Giuliani turned a deaf ear to pleas from his faithful wife to reconcile while shacking up with a woman decades his junior. And then there's William "Ace" Bennett, a man so despondent over the declining state of morals in our times that he forearmed aside an enormous pile of poker chips—even *I* don't deny his talent—to bang out a book right there in his favorite casino. Let's see, what was the title? *The Virtuous Bookie? The Death of Virtuous Gambling? Gambling with Virtue? Gambling for Virtue? Gambling As Virtue: A Metaphysical Study? The Proper Care and Feeding of Fruit Machines? A Virtuous Gent Does Vegas on Credit? Give Credit to Virtue in Vegas? Atlantic City Sunrise: Parking Lot Epiphanies? Was It Virtuous to Deal Me This Hand, Pal?* (Sometimes the ol' memory gets spotty). "'Be careful,' Jesus said to them. 'Be on your guard against the yeast of the Pharisees and Sadducees'" (Matthew 16:6).

Isn't there a measure of irony in decrying Political Correctness while White House officials harshly berate an editor for a published article and darkly warn all citizens to watch what we say? Had Pres. Bush watched what he said in the months before 9/11 about urgent warnings of imminent attack, had he not arrogantly ignored Clinton Administration holdover Richard Clarke, had he carefully guarded what passed his lips about state-sponsored terrorism and the joys of spending August on the ranch, perhaps thousands of lives could've been saved and our freedoms wouldn't have gone down the drain without touching the sides.

If Bill Clinton had spent his entire term getting pleasured by young fillies, contemptuously dismissed Republican viewpoints on national security, delayed urgent meetings for months and repeatedly warned naysayers of the ominous threat posed by Bangladesh, would liberal Democrats have gone along with this? Nor do I recall hearing Democrats dismiss the Oval Office fellatio as a sorority prank of Lewinsky's.

My last example of Pharisaism never took to heart the meaning of "Blessed is the man who does not . . . sit in the seat of mockers" (Psalm 1:1). Although Sean Hannity is sincerely angry (and justifiably so) with those who use Islam as a tool for murder, his latest book does precisely the same thing by invoking the Lord's Prayer in the service of violence. (By the way, how could he possibly be displeased with murdering abortion doctors in the name of God? After all, according to him, the end justifies the means. But this is a godless approach to ending abortion). He's an extremely busy man so I went ahead and Hannitized the Lord's Prayer for him.

The Lord's Prayer, Hannitized

Our national Good Luck Charm who is in heaven,
We blaspheme Your name in cities and towns[203],
And can't hear rebukes from left-winger clowns.
Our kingdom come, our will be done
On earth and—if You don't mind—in heaven.
We'll earn our bread today as before
And model ourselves to inspire the poor.
Forgive us our debts,
As we punish our debtors[204].
And lead us not into temptation
For we've already got the hang of it.
We've changed Your (stateside) law to prohibit
Adultery and non-political murder—that's it!!
And though we walk through the valley of the shadow of death,
We shall fear no evil, for we're the meanest S.O.B.'s in the valley[205].
*Now **SHUT** your **PIE HOLE, WORLD** and **SUBMIT***
While we deliver ourselves from evil
For ours is the kingdom and the power and the glory . . . for now. Amen[206].

"Be on your guard against the yeast of the Pharisees, which is hypocrisy" (Luke 12:1).

My heartfelt wish throughout my book was that my enthusiasm for the Bible would be infectious. Boccaccio, echoing Pope Gregory the Great, praised the Bible as follows: "It possesses openly that by virtue of which it may nourish little children, and preserves in secret that whereby it holds rapt in admiration the minds of sublime thinkers. Thus it is like a river, if I may use the figure, wherein the little lamb may wade, and the great elephant freely swim[207].

Long ago I awoke from the only bad dream I've ever had in my life. I was profoundly grieved as I sat on the edge of my bed. I've always been more deeply affected by ideas than images and as it is during the day—I hesitate to say 'in real life' because dreams, too, are real in their own way, aren't they?—so it was that night. It wasn't what I saw that got to me; indeed the images had already vanished. The import of the dream, that the last five years of my life were a complete waste, no human being could've consoled me about, even if I'd not been unattached and alone then. But I cried out to God right then and immediately He comforted me. In the decades gone by since, He kindly kept such crushing grief away but gently reminds me often of a certain story:

"'Again, [the kingdom of God] will be like a man going on a journey, who called his servants and entrusted his property to them. To one he gave five talents of money, to another two talents, and to another one talent, each according to his ability. Then he went on his journey. The man who had received the five talents went at once and put his money to work and gained five more. So also, the one with the two talents gained two more. But the man who had received the one talent went off, dug a hole in the ground and hid his master's money.

'After a long time the master of those servants returned and settled accounts with them. The man who had received the five talents brought the other five. 'Master,' he said, 'you entrusted me with five talents. See, I have gained five more.'

'His master replied, 'Well done, good and faithful servant! You have been faithful with a few things; I will put you in charge of many things. Come, and share your master's happiness!'

'The man with the two talents also came. 'Master,' he said, 'you entrusted me with two talents; see, I have gained two more.'

'His master replied, 'Well done, good and faithful servant! You have been faithful with a few things; I will put you in charge of many things. Come and share your master's happiness!'

'Then the man who had received the one talent came. 'Master,' he said, 'I knew that you are a hard man, harvesting where you have not sown and gathering where you have not scattered seed. So I was afraid and went out and hid your talent in the ground. See, here is what belongs to you.'

'His master replied, 'You wicked, lazy servant! So you knew that I harvest where I have not sown and gather where I have not scattered seed? Well then, you should have put my money on deposit with the bankers, so that when I returned I would have received it back with interest.

'Take the talent from him and give it to the one who has the ten talents. For everyone who has will be given more, and he will have an abundance. Whoever does not have, even what he has will be taken from him. And throw that worthless servant outside, into the darkness, where there will be weeping and gnashing of teeth'" (Matthew 25:14-30).

I've tried to use my talent, "the ability to distinguish between spirits" (I Corinthians 12:10), in this diatribe against the Spirit of the Age that came wafting into our midst, stealthily, propelled by the fumes rising up from the place wherein dwells the Evil One, the father of lies and murder.

It's depressing how often Christians are gulled and used by posers with a nice line in religious patois. Many of us can't even name the contents of the ten commandments monument, let alone discern the presence of crafty wolves among the flock who're adept at sprinkling their talk with code words torn from the Bible out of context. Eager to witness—or even induce—the fulfillment of Bible prophecy, we ignore wise and pious counsellors.

"A warning too I have to give, not idly, but because comparing recent and ancient events, I anticipate a great danger, unless we are on guard against it. Hopes based on some interpretation of divine prophecy are no lawful cause for war. For besides the fact that oracles which are not yet fulfilled can hardly be interpreted with certainty without the aid of the prophetic spirit, even the times of events that are sure to happen may be hidden from us. And finally, a prediction, unless it is accompanied by an express command from God, does not confer a right, for God often allows his predicted designs to be accomplished by wicked men or evil acts."[208]

Zeal for God is often not accompanied by intimate acquaintance with His Word and character. Look beneath the surface talk into the heart of a person, as He does. "I am sending you out like sheep among wolves. Therefore be as shrewd as snakes and as innocent as doves" (Matthew 10:16). "Wisdom will save you from the ways of wicked men . . . whose paths are crooked and who are devious in their ways" (Proverbs 2:12,15). "To the faithful you show yourself faithful, to the blameless you show yourself blameless, to the pure you show yourself pure, but to the crooked you show yourself shrewd" (II Samuel 22:26-27). Christ's return may come as a surprise because so many of His followers will be working for the losing side unawares.

"To hear God's 'Well done' is the most innocent and most cleansing of ambitions"[209]. As Coleridge lay dying, he said: "For, as God hears me, the originating, continuing, and sustaining wish and design in my heart was to exalt the glory of his name; and, which is the same thing in other words, to promote the improvement of mankind"[210]. This, too, is my goal.

Will you listen to the cocksure, boastful, self-righteous voices around you, or to the gentle voice of another?

> "Truth needs not the service of passion; [indeed] nothing so disserves it, as passion when set to serve it. The *Spirit of truth* is . . . the *Spirit of meekness*. The Dove that rested on that great champion of truth, who is The Truth itself, is from Him derived to the lovers of truth, and they ought to seek the participation of it. Imprudence makes some . . . Christians lose much of their labor, in speaking for religion, and drive those further off, whom they would draw into it.
>
> The confidence that attends a Christian's belief makes the believer not fear men, to whom he answers, but still he fears his God, for whom he answers, and whose interest is chief in those things he speaks of. The soul that hath the deepest sense of spiritual things, and the truest knowledge of God, is most afraid to miscarry in speaking of Him, most tender and wary how to acquit itself when engaged to speak of and for God"[211].

St. Augustine eloquently spoke of the church universal in these stirring words:

> "This heavenly city then, while it sojourns on earth, calls citizens out of all nations and gathers together a society of pilgrims of all languages, not scrupling about diversities in the manners, laws and institutions whereby earthly peace is secured and maintained, but recognizing that, however various these are, they all tend to one and the same end of earthly peace"[212].

Stand back as Goliath falls!

ENDNOTES

1   Gerard Van Groningen, quoted in Dale Ralph Davis, *Looking on the Heart, Volume 2, Expositions of I Samuel 15-31*, Baker Books, 1994, p. 105.

2   ibid.

3   ibid., p. 106.

4   ibid., p. 108, footnote 10.

5   Everett F. Harrison in *The Expositor's Bible Commentary, Vol. 10*, ed. Frank E. Gaebelein, Zondervan Publishing House, 1976, p. 139. References to this particular volume of the series hereafter cited as *The Expositor's Bible Commentary*.

6   *Crises of the Republic*, Hannah Arendt, Harvest Books, 1972, p. 177.

7   *Gulliver's Travels*, Part IV, Chapter IV.

8   *The Conservative Mind from Burke to Eliot*, Russell Kirk, Seventh Edition, Regnery Books, 1986, p. 314.

9   "Sparks of the Tempest," *Point of Know Return*, Kansas.

10 *Gulliver's Travels*, Part IV, Chapter V.

11 *The New York Review of Books*, July 3, 2003, p. 38. References to this magazine hereafter cited as *New York Review*.

12 *The Conservative Mind from Burke to Eliot*, op. cit., pp. 8-9.

13 *Leap of Faith: Memoirs of an Unexpected Life*, Queen Noor, Miramax, 2003.

14 *New York Review*, April 10, 2003, pp. 90-91.

15 James Montgomery Boice in *The Expositor's Bible Commentary*, p. 498.

16 ibid., p. 496.

17 Everett Harrison, *The Expositor's Bible Commentary*, p. 26.

18 *New York Review*, June 12, 2003, p. 22.

19 ibid.

20 *New York Review*, March 27, 2003, p. 21.

21 James Montgomery Boice, *The Expositor's Bible Commentary*, p. 498.

22 *New York Review*, June 12, 2003, p. 22.

23 *New York Review*, March 27, 2003, p. 22.

24 *Technology Review*, September 2003, pp. 76-78.

25 Reprinted in *New York Review*, April 10, 2003, pp. 91-92. Emphasis added.

26 *The Boston Globe Magazine*, April 27, 2003.

27 *New York Review*, March 25, 2004, p. 38.

28 *New York Review*, June 12, 2003, pp. 75-78.

29 ibid., p. 28.

30 ibid., p. 75.

31 ibid., p. 74.

32 ibid.

33 *New York Review*, March 27, 2003, p. 9.

34 *New York Review*, June 12, 2003, p. 80.

35 *New York Review*, March 27, 2003, p. 8. See "Global Anti-Semitism" at *www.adl.org/anti_semitism/anti-semitism_global_incidents.asp*, and "ADL Audit: Anti-Semitic Incidents Rise Slightly in US in 2000" at *www.adl.org/ presrele/asus_12/3776_12.asp*.

36 For fair-minded news sources on Middle East affairs, see The Economist (www.economist.com) and *Washington Report on Middle East Affairs* (*www.wrmea.com*).

37 *New York Review*, March 27, 2003, p. 8. See "Differences over the Arab-Israeli Conflict," *www.worldviews.org/detailreports/compreport/html/ch3s3.html*.

38 *New York Review*, June 12, 2003, p. 78.

39 *New York Review*, April 10, 2003, p. 91.

40 Hamlet wisely said: "reason panders will."

41 *New York Review*, June 12, 2003, p. 74.

42 *New York Review*, March 13, 2003, p. 20.

43 *New York Review*, May 29, 2003, p. 16.

44 Conversation described by Michael Massing, *New York Review*, March 25, 2004, p. 46.

45 *New York Review*, May 29, 2003, pp. 17, 19.

46 *New York Review*, June 12, 2003, p. 74.

47 *New York Review*, April 10, 2003, pp. 31, 75.

48 *A Theological Interpretation of American History*, C. Gregg Singer, Presbyterian and Reformed Publishing Co, 1964, p. 41. Hereafter cited as Singer.

49 Singer, p. 31.

50 *The Columbia History of Western Philosophy*, ed. Richard H. Popkin, MJF Books, 1999, p. 471. Hereafter cited as Popkin.

51 *'A Few Bloody Noses': The Realities and Mythologies of the American Revolution*, Robert Harvey, Overlook Press, 2001. Hereafter cited as Harvey.

52 Harvey, p. 349; see also p. 4.

53 ibid., p. 48.

54   ibid., p. 54.

55   ibid., p. 48.

56   Popkin, pp. 441-444.

57   Harvey, p. 57.

58   Harvey, p. 58.

59   Singer, p. 40.

60   Harvey, p. 105.

61   Harvey, p. 58.

62   ibid., pp. 355, 356-357.

63   *The New York Public Library American History Desk Reference*, eds. Marilyn
      Miller and Marian Faux, Macmillan Press, 1997, pp. 7ff. Hereafter cited as
      Miller and Faux.

64   Harvey, p. 349.

65   Harvey, p. 355.

66   Miller and Faux, p. 25.

67   Miller and Faux, pp. 107, 109.

68   David Levering Lewis, *New York Review*, November 21, 2002, p. 27.

69   Miller and Faux, p. 101.

70   *New York Review*, November 21, 2002, p. 28.

71   Miller and Faux, ibid.

72   *New York Review*, ibid.

73   Harvey, pp. 353-354.

74   Harvey, p. 344.

75   ibid., p. 353.

76   ibid., p. 356.

77   ibid., p. 145.

78   ibid., p. 428.

79   *The Strange Career of Jim Crow*, C. Vann Woodward, 2nd ed., Oxford
      University Press, 1966, p. 43. Hereafter cited as Woodward.

80   Woodward, pp. 69, 70.

81   Miller and Faux, p. 107.

82   Harvey, p. 183.

83   Harvey, p. 184.

84   ibid., p. 364.

85   ibid., p. 362.

86   *The Oxford Companion to the Supreme Court of the United States*, ed. Kermit
      L. Hall, Oxford University Press, 1992, p. 794. Hereafter cited as Hall.

87   Hall, p. 320.

[88] *The Economist*, July 12, 2003, p. 9.

[89] *New York Review*, April 8, 2004, p. 85. "To crush underfoot all prisoners in the land, to deny a man his rights before the Most High, to deprive a man of justice—would not the Lord see such things?" (Lamentations 3:34-36)

[90] Quoted by Emma Rothschild, Professor of History and Fellow of King's College, Cambridge University, in an essay entitled "Empire Beware!" in the *New York Review*, March 25, 2004, pp. 37-38. Material in single quotation marks is Madison's own words. A longer version of her essay, with footnotes, is available at *www.nybooks.com* and definitely repays careful attention.

[91] ibid., pp. 37, 38.

[92] *Gulliver's Travels*, Part IV, Chapter V.

[93] *The Economist*, June 21, 2003, pp. 26-27.

[94] Miller and Faux, p. 25.

[95] Miller and Faux, p. 23.

[96] Spoken of John Eliot in Cotton Mather's *Magnalia Christi Americana: The Life of the Renowned John Eliot*.

[97] Miller and Faux, pp. 101, 107.

[98] Miller and Faux, p. 109.

[99] Woodward, pp. 17, 20.

[100] Harvey, p. 349.

[101] Harvey, pp. 354, 355.

[102] Miller and Faux, p. 48.

[103] Harvey, p. 47.

[104] Harvey, p. 22.

[105] Miller and Faux, p. 66.

[106] Harvey, p. 93.

[107] Harvey, p. 97.

[108] ibid., p. 99.

[109] ibid., p. 160.

[110] ibid., p. 427.

[111] ibid., pp. 4, 54.

[112] ibid., pp. 6, 280.

[113] Miller and Faux, p. 20.

[114] Harvey, p. 368.

[115] Harvey, p. 364.

[116] ibid., p. 58.

[117] Miller and Faux, p. 110.

[118] Woodward, p. 21.

119   Miller and Faux, p. 109.

120   *The Economist*, June 14, 2003, p. 27.

121   *The Expositor's Bible Commentary*, pp. 26-27.

122   Harvey, pp. 2-3.

123   *Samuel Taylor Coleridge*, The Oxford Authors Series, ed. H.J. Jackson, Oxford University Press, 1985, p. 699, endnote to line 323 of the poem *Religious Musings*. Hereafter cited as Jackson.

124   Aphorism 40 quoted in *Aids to Reflection*, Samuel Taylor Coleridge, Chelsea House, 1983, p. 77. This is an edited reprint of the 1884 George Bell and Sons edition of the work. Hereafter cited by aphorism number.

125   Aphorism 39, pp. 76-77, *Aids to Reflection*.

126   *Bonifacius*, Part Eleven. Emphasis added.

127   Jackson, pp. 13ff.

128   *might*: power.

129   *passions*: eg, anger, lust. *cares*: worldly things.

130   *him except aught to desire*: to desire anything else but him.

131   *lusts*: eg, the lust for revenge.

132   "Make sure there is no man or woman, clan or tribe among you today whose heart turns away from the Lord our God to go and worship [other] gods; make sure there is no root among you that produces such bitter poison. When such a person hears the words of this oath [to follow God], he invokes a blessing on himself and therefore thinks, 'I will be safe, even though I persist in going my own way' . . . The Lord will never be willing to forgive him; his wrath and zeal will burn against that man" (Deuteronomy 29:18-20). "Do not merely listen to the word, and so deceive yourselves. Do what it says" (James 1:22).

133   *Lazar-house*: a hospital for lepers. Coleridge's lines designate specific social evils that are consequences of war: poverty that leads to crime; prostitution; neglect and starvation; forced enlistment; increasing numbers of widows and orphans.

134   *corse*: corpse.

135   "When he opened the fifth seal, I saw under the altar the souls of those who had been slain because of the word of God and the testimony they had maintained. They called out in a loud voice, 'How long, Sovereign Lord, holy and true, until you judge the inhabitants of the earth and avenge our blood?'" (Revelation 6:9-10).

136   *A History of the Arab Peoples*, Albert Hourani, Belknap Press, 1991, pp. 144-145.

137 *One Palestine, Complete: Jews and Arabs under the British Mandate*, Tom Segev, Metropolitan Books, 2000. Hereafter cited as Segev.

138 Segev, p. 43.

139 Segev, pp. 70, 71.

140 ibid., pp. 105, 106.

141 ibid., pp. 20, 104.

142 ibid., p. 407.

143 ibid., p. 404.

144 ibid.

145 ibid., p. 406.

146 Quoted in the *New York Review*, December 19, 2002.

147 Segev, pp. 455, 456.

148 Segev, p. 385.

149 ibid., p. 456.

150 ibid., pp. 456-457.

151 ibid., pp. 476, 479, 7, 502, 507.

152 ibid., pp. 454, 471.

153 Unpublished autobiography, quoted in Segev, p. 475 footnote.

154 *New York Review*, July 3, 2003, p. 8. See also Jonathan Cook, "A 1,000-Kilometer Fence Preempts the Road Map," *International Herald Tribune*, May 27, 2003.

155 Segev, pp. 136, 502.

156 Segev, p. 115.

157 ibid., p. 503.

158 ibid., p. 465.

159 ibid., pp. 9, 497.

160 Murray J. Harris, *The Expositor's Bible Commentary*, p. 353.

161 *Current History*, November 2002, p. 362. URL: *www.currenthistory.com*. All references hereafter to *Current History* are to the November 2002 issue.

162 P.W. Singer, *Current History*, p. 358. Hereafter cited as P.W. Singer.

163 Aphorism 28, pp. 68-69.

164 Aphorism 33, pp. 71-72.

165 Augustus Richard Norton, *Current History*, p. 378. Hereafter cited as Norton. A Zogby poll of Muslim attitudes is summarized at *www.zogby.com/features/features.dbm?ID=141*.

166 *New York Review*, July 3, 2003, p. 39.

167 *New York Review*, June 12, 2003, p. 28.

168 Popkin, p. 143.

169 Roxanne L. Euben, "Jihad and Political Violence," *Current History*, p. 370. Hereafter cited as Euben. The language in square brackets is my own reworking of Euben's definition of jahiliyya to bring out more clearly the area of agreement between Christianity and Islam.

170 Euben, ibid.

171 Aphorism 31, p. 70.

172 Murray Harris, *The Expositor's Bible Commentary*, p. 356.

173 Norton, p. 378.

174 "A Survey of Central Asia," *The Economist*, July 26, 2003, p.5.

175 "A Survey of Islam and the West," *The Economist*, September 13, 2003, pp. 8, 16.

176 Norton, p. 378.

177 P.W. Singer, pp. 356, 360.

178 *New York Review*, July 3, 2003, p.13.

179 P.W. Singer, p.357.

180 Aphorism 29, p. 69.

181 Euben, p. 367.

182 Euben, p. 374.

183 Aphorism 32, pp. 70-71.

184 Euben, p. 365 footnote.

185 "A Survey of Islam and the West," op. cit., p. 15.

186 Quoted in Norton, p. 381. *Toward an Islamic Reformation: Civil Liberties, Human Rights, and International Law*, Abdullahi an-Naim, Syracuse University Press, 1990. Page reference for this quotation unsupplied.

187 Norton, p. 378.

188 Euben, pp. 366, 374.

189 Euben, pp. 367, 368.

190 ibid., p. 371.

191 ibid., p. 369 footnote. See *Understanding Islam: An Introduction to the Muslim World*, Thomas W. Lippman, Mentor Books, 1990, p. 113.

192 Euben, pp. 369, 371. Mawdudi and Qutb considered that 'modernity' in both its meanings, that is, Western hegemony and spiritual ignorance, fit together hand in glove, but it was the reach of modernity that warranted a call to arms.

193 ibid., p. 369. See Abdulaziz A. Sachedina, "The Development of 'Jihad' in Islamic Revelation and History" in *Cross, Crescent, and Sword*, James Turner Johnson and John Kelsay, eds. Greenwood Press, 1990, p. 37.

194 Euben, p. 369. *War and Peace in the Law of Islam*, Majid Khadduri, Johns Hopkins University Press, 1955, pp. 65-66, 74-80.

195 Euben, p. 369.

196 ibid., p. 375 footnote. See *The Political Language of Islam*, Bernard Lewis, University of Chicago Press, 1988, pp. 2-3.

197 Euben, pp. 374-375. See Hannah Arendt, "Religion and Politics" in *Essays in Understanding: 1930-1954*, Harcourt Brace, 1994, p. 383.

198 Euben, p. 375. None of the quoted matter in this or the preceding paragraph are Arendt's own words, but rather Euben's summary. See the "Religion and Politics" essay, op. cit.

199 Euben, p. 376. See William Connolly, "Democracy and Territoriality" in *Rhetorical Republic*, Frederick M. Dolan and Thomas L. Dumm, eds., University of Massachusetts Press, 1993, p. 251.

200 Euben, ibid.

201 True confessions: I made this one up.

202 *linnet*: a small songbird that symbolizes cheerfulness.

203 See Deuteronomy 29: 18-20, op. cit., endnote 132.

204 "For if you forgive men when they sin against you, your heavenly Father will also forgive you. But if you do not forgive men their sins, your Father will not forgive your sins" (Matthew 6:14-15).

205 Obviously, Hannity loves his country deeply. We can assume that, in the heat of his passionate peroration, he inserted his rendition of Psalm 23:4 here, completely by accident. The Biblical text reads: "Even though I walk through the valley of the shadow of death, I will fear no evil, for you are with me; your rod and your staff, they comfort me."

206 Here is the original Lord's Prayer on which Hannity bases his Declaration of Independence from God. Note the humble request for God to deliver us from evil: "Our Father in heaven, hallowed be your name, your kingdom come, your will be done on earth as it is in heaven. Give us today our daily bread. Forgive us our debts, as we also have forgiven our debtors. And lead us not into temptation, but deliver us from the evil one, for yours is the kingdom and the power and the glory forever. Amen." (Matthew 6:9-13).

207 Giovanni Boccaccio, *The Life of Dante*.

208 Hugo Grotius, *The Law of War and Peace*, trans. by Louise R. Loomis, Book Two, Chapter 22, Section 15. Grotius (1583-1645), a Dutch Christian, is known as the father of international law.

209 *Ezra and Nehemiah: An Introduction and Commentary*, Derek Kidner, Inter-Varsity Press, 1979, p. 130.

210 Jackson, p. 603.

211 Aphorism 42, p. 79.

212 St. Augustine, *The City of God*.

We represent Mr. Ivey's legal affairs. Our firm has a well-earned reputation for taking aggressive measures to defend our clients. We eat red meat while it's still breathing. But we wish to deny categorically having had any part in the untimely demise of Jimmy Hoffa after he made trouble for a client of ours.

—Sue Early for the law firm of Jerp Perp Kanche Seemer and Kuhkaluhker

. . . . W-H-I-N-N-Y . . . . well hello there Zeke . . . . SWAT didn't realize my window was open . . . WAP how ya doin' today champ? . . . SWAT o-h-h-h stop that . . . your whiskers are WAP ticklin' me . . . . SWAT THUMP hmmm that explains all the flies . . . . woops, knocked my memoirs off the desk . . . .

You want me ta read a BOOK?!! A book without PICTURES?! . . . . Get outta here! . . . no no not YOU mate, the [confounded] pony . . . . What [clown] let the [libidinal] pony in the house? . . . . Get out!! . . . [Holy guacamole] Stay away from me [sexually active] statue! . . . Shoo, Baxter! [Awww bejabbers! Dadgumit!] he [dropped a load-and-a-half] on me [loose-moraled] boots. Will you look at the size of this [problem]? He buried me [bloomin'] snakeskin boots!! You sorry [critter what mates rather frequently] . . . . [Blimey] stop running so fast, Baxter. Whoa, I landed in the [bad patch]. No-o-o-o [gee willikers] not the [bloody] **CRASH** statue!! [Pitch me naked into a brier patch] Jack! Kelly! [Mule feathers!] I think I bruised me [doggone] kidney when I fell. *Jack*!! *Kelly*!! And that's me good one. (Sigh). Now how will I pee? . . . Wouldja mind rollin' the paramedics, mate? J-A-A-C-K!!! K-E-E-E-L-L-Y!!!

—Ozzy Osbourne

. . . . well . . . . uhm . . . . ah-h-h . . . . the . . . uh . . . . ahem . . . well I have to admit the book does SMELL purdy.

—Sonny Moman, *Crawford (Tex.) Chronicle*

www.ingramcontent.com/pod-product-compliance
Lightning Source LLC
Chambersburg PA
CBHW020345260626
47156CB00004B/1688